THE DEADLY HOMECOMING

A Red Badge Novel of Suspense

by THEODORE GEORGE

DODD, MEAD & COMPANY
NEW YORK

ISBN: 0-396-06656-9
Library of Congress Catalog Card Number: 72-3918
Printed in the United States of America
by Vail-Ballou Press, Inc., Binghamton, N. Y.

THE DEADLY HOMECOMING

Also by Theodore George

THE MURDERS ON THE SQUARE

1706260

THE DEADLY HOMECOMING

CHAPTER 1

ARNOLD ZIMMERMAN was thinking about the hot-box torture chamber in *The Bridge on the River Kwai* as he instinctively tried to get his balance in the lurching, overheated subway car. As it was, he was held in place by the people squeezed in beside him, so that he did not fall even though his contact with the floor was restricted to the ball of one foot and the toe of the other. He lurched against an overwhelmingly fat woman as the train slowed sharply, and before he could pull himself away, he felt himself sinking into her bovine bosom. Although any sexual motivation was the farthest thing from his mind, the ungainly embrace earned him a look that could have sunk a battleship.

"Kaahway" the staticky speaker announced. If he had not taken this ride every day for more years than he cared to recount, he never would have been able to discern that the conductor had just declared that the station was Kings Highway.

Struggling to get to the side of the car where the doors were beginning to slide open, Zimmerman wedged himself into a flank of other passengers seeking similar escape. Together they burst forth from the door onto the platform, spurting out of the car like pus from a pimple. At least a dozen people had disembarked, yet the car looked just as crowded as it pulled out of the station.

Without thinking, he fell into step with the other pas-

1

sengers in their descent from the elevated station to the street. As he left the protection of the lean-to adjacent to the platform and went down to the first landing of the stairs, he was accosted by a cool breeze from the wide avenue beneath him. The heat of the August day, which had been retained in the subway car, had broken on the Brooklyn streets with the twilight. The breeze that had resulted now plastered his sweat-soaked shirt against his body like a cold compress. He shivered involuntarily.

Emerging thankfully onto the sidewalk, he paused at the newsstand located next to the station and purchased the earliest edition of tomorrow morning's *News*. As he stood in the stall waiting for his change, he took out a handkerchief to wipe the perspiration from his face. Although he was chilled, rivulets of sweat continued to flow freely from his forehead and neck. He looked at the clean, neatly folded handkerchief thoughtfully and decided not to use it. Instead, he fumbled through his pockets until he found some crumpled Kleenex. Mopping his brow and the back of his neck, he returned the soggy mass of tissue to his pocket. The antilitterbug advertising campaigns had had their effect.

The news dealer returned and handed him his change. Instinctively turning to the racing results in the newspaper, he glanced at the tally sheets. Reckoning quickly, he estimated that he had lost $110.

On any other day, this realization would have upset him enough to require that he stop for at least one drink before going home. But today he merely shrugged, as if he had expected it, and continued the walk to his house. In a way he felt relieved. The world had not changed, and his analysis of his lot in life had been accurate. He was a loser and he knew it. Somehow, he took comfort in it. It was rather like searching for a hollow tooth with your tongue and not being disappointed when you felt the pain on finding it.

Turning the corner to his block, he surveyed his neighbors' homes and his own house in the distance. All alike. Built in pairs like Siamese twins, each semidetached brick house had exactly the same face. From time to time one of the block's residents had decided to make his house a little different by installing shutters or repainting the door, or even, in one case, painting the bricks white. But the same thing always happened. The fellow who lived in the other half of the structure had not gone along with the idea and had left his own home as it was. The half-white house had been a local joke until the paint wore off and the building had returned to its original condition. When the new shutters came loose they were not replaced, and when it was time to repaint the front door, the owner carefully chose a color that matched that of his neighbor.

Ordinarily, this sight would have depressed Zimmerman, who thought of himself as something of an aesthete. But today, he saw only the beauty of the trees in full leaf and of the neatly cut postage-stamp front lawns.

As he passed his neighbors' homes, he saw that each had a television set holding its prey in togetherness. Windows were open in those houses without air-conditioners, and a clatter of night baseball rose and fell to the drone of humming air coolers, hitting the street in waves whenever the home team got a hit.

He felt curiously calm, calmer than he could ever remember. He was as much at peace with himself as if he had paid all his bills. Just before he reached his house, he looked carefully around him, peering at each of his nearby neighbors' windows. All he could see was the reflected gray of television screens. He glanced in each of the cars at the sidewalk. They were all unoccupied and at rest for the night. Years of dodging bill collectors and bookmakers' "agents" had trained him to be observant. No headlights were in sight, and the only visible movement on the street was the shadows of the trees as they moved in the light of the streetlight on the corner. He ascended the brick steps of his stoop and paused at the door.

The gun barrel felt cold at the base of his skull where head joined neck. If he had had time to think about it, he would have acknowledged that he was terrified. The visual impression of a great flash of light was the last thing he perceived. He was dead before the 9 mm. Luger explosion had time to route itself from his eardrum to his brain.

CHAPTER 2

THE TELEPHONE WAS ringing irritably as Alfred Zimmerman inserted the key into his front-door lock. And, as he had anticipated, as soon as he got the door open and entered the apartment, leaving both the suitcases and his wife standing in the hallway, the persistent ringing ceased.

Muttering to himself, he turned back to assist his wife, who had begun to haul the heavy leather luggage into the living room.

"They don't even wait for me to get home," he complained as he hefted two large two-suiters and carried them in from the hall. "Where do you want these, Kathy?"

"Oh, just put them down anywhere. I'll unpack them tomorrow. I'm too exhausted to start now."

Zimmerman deposited them where he stood next to the couch and returned to the hallway to retrieve the rest of the load.

"If you don't mind," he said as he set down the last of the luggage they had brought up from the garage, "I think I'll leave the rest of the stuff in the trunk of the car for now. I can get up early tomorrow and bring it up before I go to work."

"Oh, sure," she replied. "And it will still be in the car for our next vacation. If you don't do it now, there's no telling when it might get done."

"Oh, hell, Kathy," he said peevishly, "you know I'm tired. You didn't have to drive."

5

"Come on, Al," Kathy prodded gently. "If you get everything in now, then I can unpack it all tomorrow. Besides, it's not really all that safe in the car overnight, even if the car is in the garage."

"Well, it is locked in the trunk," he countered weakly, knowing that he was defeated. "No one's going to break into the trunk."

"Sure," she answered. "So somebody will steal the car."

He had already turned and was heading for the door when she called, "Thanks, Al. If whoever that was on the phone calls back, I'll take a message."

Pausing in the doorway, he turned his head and told her, "If it's my office, tell them I'll be in on time in the morning. I don't care if Jack the Ripper is on the loose; I'm just too tired to play policeman tonight."

Detective Lieutenant Alfred Zimmerman was puffing audibly as he unloaded the elevator at his floor in the apartment house. One duffel bag, one cardboard carton filled with dishes, two folding Valpaks, and a tacklebox already sprawled across the terrazzo hallway floor. A mechanical voice intoned: "Stand clear of the doors, please. Please do not block the elevator. Please take the next elevator." He glanced at the carton he was using to hold the door ajar to make sure it was securely jamming the sliding door open. The voice (the same girl, no doubt, who makes recordings for the phone company: "I'm sorry, you have reached a non-working number") had always got on his nerves. Being as tired as he was, the effect was worse tonight. Why is it, he wondered, that if men were supposed to be the symbols of authority, they always used women's voices on those recordings? Maybe, he reasoned, because they nag better. And, he thought, as he loaded the balance of their things from the elevator floor under his arms, precariously clamping a pair of canoe paddles under his armpit, they never stop until they get their way. He pushed the carton out of the door's path with his foot and allowed the door to slide shut just as the recording had recycled. "Stand clear of the . . ."

He was fumbling with the handle on one of the Valpaks, trying to build a load for himself when the door to the apartment next to his swung open. "Hey, turn that elevator loose, will you," Haggerty, his neighbor, demanded. "People are trying to sleep, you know." Haggerty stepped into the hall clad in short-pants pajamas. His fat, hairy legs gave him the appearance of a grown man ridiculously attired in a little boy's clothes for a costume party. "Oh, hello, Al. How was your vacation?" Without waiting for an answer, Haggerty declared, "I'm sure glad you're back." Zimmerman looked up. Haggerty was not really a bad neighbor, but the two men were hardly close friends. "Why's that, neighbor?" the policeman inquired.

"Your damn phone's been ringing all night, that's why."

Zimmerman managed to insert his left fingers into the handle of the other Valpak and began the short trip down the hall to his own door.

"I don't know how people are supposed to sleep when phones keep ringing every fifteen minutes. Damn cheap construction. You know these walls are made out of tissue paper. Couldn't you ask your friends to call at more reasonable times? I mean, every fifteen minutes since nine o'clock. It's been driving me crazy."

"Sorry," Zimmerman allowed for no reason other than being too tired to argue. "You better go inside, though. You'll catch cold standing on this cold floor in your bare feet." The corn plasters on Haggerty's toes completed the ridiculous image, and Zimmerman was hard put to keep from laughing.

"There! There it goes again!" Haggerty announced as a telephone ring summoned Zimmerman from the hall. "Every fifteen minutes, like clockwork. How's anybody supposed to sleep?"

7

CHAPTER 3

"WHAT?" Zimmerman heard his wife ask the caller on the phone as he deposited the baggage next to the other pieces on the living-room floor. "Please . . . I can't understand you. Slow down."

She raised her eyebrows at her husband as if to say: I don't know what's going on.

"What? Please, wait a minute and I'll put my husband on. He just walked in."

Placing her hand over the mouthpiece, she told Zimmerman, "Some woman. I think she said she's your Aunt Hilda. Do you have an Aunt Hilda? I can't understand her. She sounds very upset."

"Hinda, Aunt Hinda," Zimmerman corrected. "God, I haven't spoken to her in years. What the hell could she want?" He took the receiver.

"Hello?"

"Is that you, Allie?"

Zimmerman winced at the nickname that he hadn't heard since he was a child. He hadn't liked the name even then.

"Yes, Aunt Hinda? What's the matter?"

"Oh, Allie, how can I tell you? How can I tell you?"

"Why don't you just try?"

"It's your brother, Allie. It's Arnie."

"What, is he in trouble again? What has he done this time?" Zimmerman was relieved that it wasn't his office call-

8

ing him in on some emergency. His younger brother was always getting into some scrape or other. And they always ended up costing the policeman just about all his savings to get his brother out.

"I told him last time that he was going to have to fend for himself from now on. I'm sick and tired of paying his debts and covering his bad checks."

When their parents had been killed in an automobile accident, it had fallen upon Alfred Zimmerman, as a young patrolman of twenty-one, to support his brother and put him through college. He had accepted that obligation at the time and had done so willingly, as his brother was six years his junior and scarcely in a position to support himself. But now the lieutenant was fifty-three and his brother, forty-seven. And the baby brother had yet to show any signs of being self-sufficient. Enough was enough.

"Is that why you're calling instead of him? Is he afraid to call for himself now?" Instead of growing up, the younger Zimmerman had seemed to have regressed. On one occasion, the detective even had had to use his rather limited influence to straighten out a mess that could have resulted in criminal charges. That business had cost Al Zimmerman three years' savings, the money he and Kathy had been setting aside for a down payment on a house of their own. And that's just what it had cost to make restitution. The lieutenant still owed some favors on that matter that he might never be able to repay.

"Allie, are you sitting down? You better sit down," his aunt suggested. Her voice seemed a little calmer and more resolved now. "Allie, I've got some very bad news."

He heard her suck in her breath. Then she blurted, "Arnie's dead. He's been murdered. I'm over at his house with Barbara and the kids. Oh, Allie, it's so awful. Who could have done such a thing? Arnie . . . murdered."

Zimmerman and his wife had been looking at each other

9

when the news hit him. Although he was not aware of any change in his composure, he saw a frightened expression appear on Kathy's face as she watched him. For a long moment no one spoke, then Zimmerman said into the telephone, "I'll see you tomorrow." He replaced the receiver on its cradle and sat down in the easy chair behind him. He felt as if he had been whacked in the midsection with a hockey stick.

"What's the matter, Al?" Kathy finally asked.

At first he was unable to speak. Then, very slowly as he regained his presence, he told her.

"My brother's been murdered."

There was nothing she could say but "Oh . . . ."

CHAPTER 4

ZIMMERMAN HAD BEEN at the other end of his spectrum of emotion many times, As a detective lieutenant attached to Manhattan Homicide South, it had frequently fallen on him to carry the grim news to the wives and families of people who had left for work in the morning and would never return, but his long experience with death had done absolutely no good in preparing him for what he now felt. The emotional impact was so strong that he was physically sick. He became very conscious of the fact that he was breathing, and he had to deliberately inhale and exhale, as if these functions were no longer taking place automatically.

Taking him by the elbow, Kathy helped him up and led him to the bedroom. He seated himself on the edge of the bed and simply watched while she removed his shoes and loosened his belt.

"Lie down, Al," she suggested. "Can I get you anything?"

He raised his feet onto the bed. "No, nothing," he replied. She clicked off the light as she left the room.

In the dark, he stared at the ceiling while the knowledge that his brother was dead sunk in. The initial shock was wearing off now, and he began thinking about his kid brother—not as he was when they had last seen each other, some six months ago, but as he was as a child, when the two boys had been close. At night sometimes they had stared at the ceiling in the room they shared and Arnie had asked questions about everything under the sun. Being the older brother, Al had always answered with authority, even if he didn't really know.

Now he was thinking about how much his brother had changed. The curly-haired, optimistic little boy had become a balding, middle-aged failure of a man. God, Al thought, I can't even think about him without automatically reminding myself that he was a failure. But maybe that was so deep in his character that it was impossible to think of him otherwise. He conjured up an image of his brother as a man. Defeat seemed to seep from his pores, exuding an aura of depression. Even when Arnie had worn one of his custom-made suits—"You can't be successful unless you look successful"—he always looked as if he had bought it slightly used or had rented it for the occasion. Whenever Al saw him he was wearing a new suit. And somehow the older brother always knew that the suit hadn't been paid for yet. Why the stores kept extending credit was beyond the understanding of the policeman. But as long as they did, Arnie would keep buying.

Lord, he was such a bright kid. He could have become just about anything he wanted. He had a college scholarship, but he flunked out. He just couldn't bring himself to work at anything. If he could have ever concentrated on accomplishing something, he could have done it. But his enthusiasms were as brief as they were intense. He would get all worked up about something—some business deal or some job or some project that was going to make him a million dollars. And as soon as it got a little complicated or boring; as soon as it seemed he'd have to work at it in order to make it succeed, he dropped it.

So I got him back into college, Zimmerman recalled. Not an Ivy League school this time, but one of the municipal colleges. And I stayed on his back until he graduated. He was going to be a doctor. I was supporting him, and I told him I'd go on paying his way until he was practicing.

12

But one night in the second half of his freshman year at medical school, he came home and told me that he had quit. He wasn't going to leech off me for another six years, he said. I told him not to worry about that, but he said he was going to start making a living for himself. No matter how I tried to argue him out of it, he insisted that he had made up his mind.

He took a job, then, selling fluoroscopes and diathermy machines and X-ray equipment for one of the big manufacturers. Oh, he was going to be making twenty thousand a year before he was twenty-five. You sell just one of the big X-ray things and the commission was almost two thousand bucks. If he could sell one a month, he'd be rich. And, of course, he was going to pay me back for putting him through school.

That job lasted less than six months. He sold a lot of equipment, all right, and for a while it looked as if he was going to do pretty well. But then it turned out that the machines were being returned almost as fast as he was selling them. What he was doing was promising the customers the sun, the moon, and the stars, and not delivering. Doctors would ask if the machine had a particular feature, or would do a certain job, and he always told them Yes. Even if it didn't. The machines started coming back to the manufacturer, and soon he was looking for another job.

Next he went to work for one of the pharmaceutical companies, canvassing doctors and peddling pills to them. But he discovered that he could make more on the side by selling samples to some practitioners who were not really doctors. Nothing that he could be prosecuted for, of course. He was simply keeping every quack in Brooklyn supplied with medicines that he should have been giving away to legitimate doctors. So that job didn't last very long, either.

And after that . . . after that he got some other job. The elder Zimmerman couldn't remember what it was.

And Arnie met Barbara and got married and he was still going to conquer the world. One thing about that kid, he never lost faith. He was always going to make a killing on his next deal, and the streets in front of his house were going to be paved in gold. The down payment on his house, by the way, had been a wedding present from his in-laws.

And then they lost touch. Arnie was busy hustling one deal or another, and his big brother was working twelve hours a day plus studying for sergeant's exams, and then he got married himself. So for the last . . . God, it's twenty years . . . the two brothers had seen each other no more than once or twice a year. When Arnie needed money. Or Arnie needed a favor. Or Arnie had some new deal cooking that required two men to run it. Even as late as last year, he had a scheme worked out that was going to make both of them rich.

Zimmerman smiled. He never quit, that kid.

And now he was dead. Zimmerman sighed audibly and looked at the clock by the side of the bed. It was five thirty in the morning and he'd have to get up in forty-five minutes to go to work. Work? Not today, he reminded himself. Today was for going to Brooklyn and burying the dead.

Knowing that less than an hour of sleep would be worse than no sleep at all, Zimmerman rose from the bed and went to the kitchen to make some coffee. On his way through the living room he saw his wife asleep in a chair. Around her were clothes from the suitcases she had begun to unpack and to sort for replacement into closets and drawers. Quietly, he pulled a hassock up to her feet and lifted her legs onto it to make her more comfortable.

Proceeding to the kitchen, he put a kettle of water on the stove to boil; then headed for the bathroom to shave. Glancing out the window, he was pleased to see that the sun was out. It has been a long night.

The simple act of getting dressed, something he had been

doing automatically for years, now took on meaning. Not only was he putting on a suit for the first time since he had left for his vacation, but he was deliberately selecting a dark-blue suit and a black tie. By force of habit, he went to his top closet shelf and removed a locked metal box. Opening it, he took out his service revolver and harness. At this point he stopped and thought about what he was doing. He was not going to work today; he was going to his dead brother's house in Brooklyn. His murdered brother. With a new sense of resolve, he strapped the harness under his left arm, so that the holster snuggled about four inches under his armpit, then buckled up and slipped the gun into place. He put on his jacket before returning to the kitchen to make his coffee.

The sight of the gun had always made Kathy uneasy. It reminded her too much of the business her husband was in, and of its risks, and even though she lay asleep in the living room, long-time habit dictated that he put on his jacket to cover the tools of his trade before breakfast. Although his pistol was as much a part of the policeman's clothing as his necktie, and considerably more important in his work, he had had to agree that firearms were out of place at the breakfast table.

When he returned to the kitchen, Zimmerman was surprised to see his wife standing there and mixing instant coffee powder into two cups of boiling water.

"Sorry I woke you," he began. "I was only trying to make you comfortable."

"No, I was up," she answered. "I was just resting my eyes."

She brought the coffee to the table, placing one cup in front of him and the other opposite. Seating herself, she asked, "What are your plans today?"

He took a long sip of the hot brew before he answered.

"I suppose first I'll go out to Arnie's house and see if

there's anything I can do for Barbara and the kids. I don't even know if anybody's arranged for the funeral yet, or called his rabbi. Knowing my family, nobody has. And he should be buried today."

She nodded. "That's one of the few Jewish traditions I really wish we Catholics would adopt. You bury the dead quickly and don't make a whole production out of it, with wakes and lying in state and all that. It's a lot more civilized your way."

He did not comment on this. The difference in their religions had rarely been a topic of conversation in the Zimmerman household, and he could not see any point in making it an issue, even in casual conversation.

"Do you want to come with me now," he asked, "or would you rather just meet me at the funeral? I can give you a call once I find out when and where it will be."

"Whatever you think best, Al. Your family might not want me there now, you know."

Zimmerman bridled. He felt a tightening sensation at the back of his neck, an anger reaction similar to a dog's hackles rising. The fact that his wife's observation might well be true annoyed him considerably.

"You're my wife, aren't you? I don't care whether your maiden name was Sullivan or Solomon." They had made their peace on the subject of religion, primarily by avoiding it. If it didn't bother them, Zimmerman couldn't see why it should upset members of their families who were nowhere near as close to it as they were. Yet it did, and he knew it. It was really something, he had observed, that the members of his family who cared the least about being Jewish, the ones who wouldn't be caught in a synagogue even on the High Holy Days, had been the ones who had disapproved of his marriage the most—including his brother, who hadn't set foot in any house of worship since his own bar mitzvah. Arnie and Barbara had eloped to Maryland to avoid that peculiarly Jewish *gemütlichkeit* that weddings often become. When the elder Zimmerman had married, selected members of both families had been invited. The only guests who showed up, however, were a handful of Zimmerman's police cronies and his bride's college roommate.

Zimmerman was tempted now to say, You're coming with me, and if they don't like it they can lump it. But thinking of his old aunts and the rest of his rather emotional tribe, he thought better of it. No sense in turning a funeral into a family battleground.

"Frankly," he finally said, "it's one of those situations where you can't win for losing. If you come with me now, I have to admit that some of my illustrious clan may look on you as an intruder. If you don't, they're going to say: Look at that girl Allie married. She can't even be a good sister-in-law and try to be a good dutiful wife and help her husband in his time of grief. You can't win either way." He shrugged his shoulders in indecision.

"By the way, Al," she asked, "how are you feeling now? You were in pretty bad shape last night."

"Oh, better, I guess. The shock of it has worn off. I'll be all right."

He looked at his wristwatch and saw that it was seven fifteen. Rising from the table, he headed for the phone in the living room.

"I better call my office and let them know that I won't be in today. Maybe they know something about what happened last night. Aunt Hinda did say that Arnie had been murdered, but she was pretty upset, and she always did exaggerate."

He returned to the kitchen a few minutes later and sat down to his refilled coffee cup. He stared at his wife thoughtfully for a moment and then revealed: "He *was* murdered. Or assassinated might be a better word. Shot through the back of the head. Brooklyn Homicide South is handling it.

17

Barbara told the investigating officer that I was a cop, so they called my office last night. They thought I'd be driving back this morning, so Brooklyn South notified the State Police and asked them to get in touch with me at the cabin. I knew we should have put in a phone out there."

Drinking his coffee quickly, he set the cup down in its saucer and rose to his feet.

"I think I'll stop off at Brooklyn South before I go to the house," he informed his wife. "You don't want to hang around there while I'm checking this out. I'll give you a call about the time and place of the funeral."

CHAPTER 5

THERE'S SOMETHING about police stations, Zimmerman thought as he walked up the concrete steps of Brooklyn South regional headquarters. They're all alike. Or at least they've all got the same feel about them. His own office was in the middle of a manufacturing and office district, and had never seemed out of place there. But Brooklyn South stood on a corner amid blocks of residences and small mom and pop stores. It was the biggest building for blocks around and stood out like a warning and a fortress to the peaceful householders. Mothers in the area would threaten their unruly children that they would be taken to the police station if they didn't behave, and the building looked so imposing compared to its surroundings that the children would be appropriately frightened. There were no children to be frightened living near Manhattan South.

But for all these differences, the buildings were similar. It was as if at some point in time in the late nineteenth century someone had decided that this was what a police station should look like, and cities across the country had been stuck with the image ever since.

Zimmerman had only been at Brooklyn South twice before in his career, years earlier, yet the atmosphere of the place was familiar. Walking through the entry room, dominated by the high sergeant's desk, he was able to head directly up the stairs and make for the detective squad room, and go through that into homicide, even though he had never been in that particular part of the building.

Zimmerman walked into his Brooklyn counterpart's office without knocking, pausing at the open door until Lieutenant Snyder waved him in and motioned for him to sit down. Snyder was arguing with someone on the telephone. Zimmerman could hear enough of the conversation to ascertain that the argument was something bureaucratic within the department. Finally, Snyder hung up in disgust.

"Do me a favor, will you, Al," the Brooklynite asked. "When you get back to your office—you know those witness' statement forms? I think they're three-o-one b's Would you send me a box or two if you've got them? We've been out of them for over a week and I can't seem to get our stationery-supplies office to send me any. They keep arguing that they just sent me six boxes, and I keep telling them that they never got here. In the meantime, all the paperwork we're sending through is bouncing back because it's not on the right forms. There are times when I don't believe this place."

Snyder did not wait for a reply. The annoyed look left his face and was replaced by an expression of grave sympathy.

"Al, how the hell do you say it? I heard about your brother, and I want you to know that we all feel pretty bad about it."

Zimmerman nodded his acknowledgment.

"I suppose you want the details," Snyder surmised. "Corey! Bring in the file on Zimmerman, Arnold W."

"Thanks, Duke," Zimmerman said. Snyder went back to the days of the Dodgers in Brooklyn, when it was difficult for any baseball fan named Snyder to escape that nickname. In this case, the name Duke fit the policeman—his Christian name was David—and so it had stuck.

"Here we go," Snyder began when the file was delivered

to him. "Zimmerman, Arnold W. Crime reported seven eighteen PM, August eleventh. Phone call from Mrs. Frank Sutter, the next-door neighbor. Officers Cotterman and Healy from the Eighty-Second Precinct arrived on the scene at seven thirty-four. Radioed us at seven forty. We dispatched detectives Blaine and Patrick—"

"Terry Patrick?" Zimmerman asked. "Good man. Worked for me for a while a few years ago."

"Yeah, he made detective second class and we got him here. Very thorough guy. Good on details . . .

"Well, Blaine and Patrick got there at seven fifty-eight. They radioed a confirmed homicide at eight-o-five and requested the meatwag——uh . . . an ambulance. Body was removed to morgue at Coney Island Hospital at nine fifty, after photographers got through."

Snyder looked up from the manila file and pushed the document across the desk to his visitor.

"That's all we've got right now. Just the preliminary report. Blaine and Patrick are still writing up their own paperwork. That should be ready sometime today. I'll be glad to give you a call when it's ready, if you want."

"No, I'll be at the funeral today. I'll call you guys probably late this afternoon," Zimmerman replied. "Let me ask you something, Duke. Have you got any feeling about this one? How does it look to you so far?"

"Well," Snyder answered after a pause, "I talked to Blaine when he got back here last night, and I did a little digging on my own through Records and Identification. Your brother was in a scrape, not so long ago, you know. . . ."

Zimmerman nodded that he knew this.

"Uh, everything considered, Al, uh . . . it doesn't look good."

"What do you mean, Duke?"

"Well, look at the pattern. You're a cop. You've seen things like this before. A guy who's in to the bookies for a bundle. Owes a couple of loan sharks around town. Lousy credit rating, even with the sharks. Only one petty arrest, and he got out of that. . . ." Snyder looked up at Zimmerman knowingly, as if to indicate that Zimmerman's police affiliation might have had something to do with his brother's release. Zimmerman averted his eyes.

"A chronic, almost compulsive gambler, and he usually lost. Then he's found on his own doorstep, nice and public, murdered in a very deliberate way.

"Come on, Al. You know as well as I do that no amateur did this job. You had a case like this yourself a while back. Every so often the racketeers decide that their nonpayers need an example of what can happen to them. This is just an educated guess at this point, of course, but it looks to me like that kind of job.

"By the way, did you ever get anybody on that case you handled? You remember the one I mean, don't you?"

"Yeah, I remember it all right. Angelo Ferroni. He worked on the docks. No, we could never even get a lead on it. Even our informants clammed up on that one. It's really something, you know. They'd turn in their own mothers, but as soon as it has anything to do with the mobs, they don't know a thing and they can't find out either.

"Do you really think that's what happened to my brother?"

"Al," Snyder said patiently, "we've both been cops for a long time. Doesn't it look that way to you?"

CHAPTER 6

As HE DROVE toward his late brother's house, Zimmerman mulled over the possibility that his brother had been assassinated by organized crime interests. And as much as he hated to admit it, the method of the crime made that seem probable. It was, indeed, typical of their executions.

A shudder of pity coursed through him as he considered the character of his brother. This feeling turned quickly to an anger of frustration, and his arms and hands began to shake so much that he had to pull over to the curb until the spasms subsided.

Accepting the fact that his brother was dead was already accomplished. Accepting the fact that he would never be able to find his murderer was something else altogether. A child stared in the open car window at him. "Hey, mister, are you all right?"

Shocked back into reality by the knowledge that he was being observed, Zimmerman quickly got hold of himself.

"Yeah, yeah, sure. I'm fine," he answered, restarting his car and pulling out into traffic. "I'm just fine," he said to no one.

The street in front of his brother's house was clogged with cars, and like Zimmerman, their drivers were looking for parking spaces. Even the driveway was blocked. Rather than circling the block, however, as the other drivers were doing, Zimmerman went straight across the next intersection and down to the next block. There he found room with no difficulty.

"Barbara," Zimmerman asked, once he succeeded in getting his sister-in-law aside and away from the solicitous neighbors and relatives, "what happened?"

"Al, please," she replied in anguish. "Not now. All I've done since it happened is answer questions. I told the police everything I knew last night. Then, this morning, two more showed up. I only just got rid of them. And now you want to ask me more questions. Just for today, Al . . . Arnie was your brother, so let's lay him to rest. Tomorrow I'll answer your questions."

Zimmerman made a mental note to check back with Synder to see if the follow-up team this morning had turned up anything different. "Barbara, I'm not going to ask you a lot of questions. Arnie *was* my brother, and I'm only asking you how he died. I think I have a right to know, don't you?"

"Al, all I can tell you is what I already told the detectives. A little after seven last night, I was waiting dinner for him to get home. I was in the kitchen. I heard an explosion and ran to the front door to see what had happened, and he was lying there."

Her body started shaking as if it were about to erupt. He put his hands on her shoulders to calm her down, and felt the waves of hysteria rising, trying to break through the surface veneer of control she had managed to maintain.

"God, it was terrible," she finally continued. "It was unreal. Like it wasn't Arnie lying there, or anybody, for that matter. It was just a body. Somebody's body. If I hadn't seen him get dressed yesterday morning, and didn't know what he was wearing, I don't think I would have recognized him. Can you believe it? I was married to that man for twenty years, and I don't think I would have

24

recognized him. It was . . . it was . . . uh . . . ghastly. His whole face was changed. And his neck! I know you're used to that kind of thing, being a cop. But I don't know how you do it. I stood there. That's all I did. I stood there and then I threw up and then I started screaming. By that time, Harriet Sutter from next door got there and she took me back into the house. I guess she called the police. I don't know how you can get used to something like that, Al. I know it's your job, but I just don't know."

"Believe me, Barbara, you never get used to it. Never," he said. "Just when you think you've finally developed a cast-iron stomach, you see one that tells you you were wrong. You're still as human and sensitive as you ever were. I'll tell you honestly, Barbara, you're taking it a lot better than most of the women I've had to do business with.

"Now let me ask you this: Did you see anybody on the street when you went out? Or anything at all out of the ordinary?"

"Out of the ordinary?" she answered sarcastically. "Yes. I saw my husband's body. Al, I'll bet I've been asked that question a dozen times since last night. And the answer is still the same. No. I didn't see anybody on the street. I wasn't looking for anybody. I was more concerned for what was lying right in front of me at my feet." She paused and gathered her wits for a moment. "No, Al. I didn't see anybody running away, if that's what you mean. And I probably would have seen something like that if anyone had been there. All I saw was Arnie."

"How long did it take for you to get to the door, Barbara?"

"I don't know. However long it takes. You know the kitchen's in the back of the house. I heard the explosion, and I guess it startled me, so I probably waited a second before I went to the front door to see what it was. Oh, I went to the window first and looked out to see if I could see anything. Then I opened the door. You can't really see too much through the window anyway. The way the foyer juts out, you can't see anything to the left of the front window. But I could see directly in front of the house, and I could see down the street to my right all the way to the corner, and I didn't see anybody at all. No cars going by, either.

"I'm sorry," she concluded, "but that's really all I know."

Zimmerman nodded. "That's okay, Barbara. I'm sorry I had to cross-examine you this way. But Arnie was my brother and I don't want to see whoever did this get away with it. I know how you feel right now because I feel the same way myself. For a long time we were pretty close, you know. Believe me, I didn't get any sleep at all last night.

"But in cases like this, time can be important. The longer we give whoever did this to cover his tracks, the less chance we have of catching him. But enough of that for now. Have you made the arrangements for the funeral? Have you called the rabbi?"

As Zimmerman had anticipated, he ended up taking care of those tasks himself.

CHAPTER 7

ORGANIZED CRIME, Zimmerman mused as he drove back to Brooklyn Homicide South, how the hell can you stop it? Or do anything about it, for that matter? It was too insidious and too widespread. It's almost like cutting open a patient to remove a tumor and discovering that the cancer has spread throughout his body. Except that Zimmerman like almost every policeman he knew, was hoping against hope that the illness wasn't terminal—that the rot could be cut away and the rest of the body would remain healthy.

He knew that wasn't too likely. Unless people changed their definitions. A speaker at a division meeting a few months back had summed it up pretty well, Zimmerman recalled. Or at least, the guy had set him to thinking.

Organized crime, this fellow had said, was as successful as it was because it catered to human weakness. Gambling, prostitution, narcotics—these were the major sources of revenue. Now, you can tell a man not to gamble and you can make it illegal, but that's not going to stop him from placing a bet. You can outlaw prostitution, but that's not going to discourage either the whores or their customers. You can tell a junky that his habit is against the law, but that isn't going to make his craving any weaker.

So what happens? Because these things are illegal, their practitioners are almost forced to organize for their mutual protection against the law.

It all started with booze during prohibition. The law

against drinking didn't make people stop wanting a drink. At first, a lot of little independents started selling their home brews and bathtub gins. And one after another, they were shut down. But for each one that was raided, a half-dozen others grew up to take its place. And they were able to succeed because they were organized. If one independent speakeasy got raided out of twenty-five in a given area, it might have served as a warning if the others were independents. But in a large organization, in which all twenty-five belonged to the same group, the raid meant only a four percent business loss. With the kind of profits that this business brought in (all tax-free, of course), the Organization could afford the gamble. Hell, oil companies faced similar risks every time they opened a gas station or drilled a well.

So before you knew it, the expert had maintained, organized crime had a choke collar on the town.

But it wasn't hopeless. Little by little, the state was closing the arteries of crime by opening those same streams to everybody else. Off-track betting had long been a major source of revenue to the Organization—until New York made it legal and regulated it. Now the bettor has no reason for going to a bookie when he can get the same opportunities from a legitimate enterprise, plus the additional knowledge that everything was aboveboard and there was no question of being paid should he hit a big winner.

It takes us a long time to learn, though. We saw the same thing with the repeal of prohibition. Once booze was legal, the criminal elements were quickly driven out of the business. In countries where prostitution is legal and government-regulated, organized crime has never been able to gain a foothold. It's sort of free enterprise at its finest, the expert had said, chuckling. If a customer-citizen is looking for a prostitute, he'd much rather go to a girl he knows has had a medical examination recently than take his chances

28

on the street. People would much rather drink at a bar with a license than run the risk of being blinded drinking questionable liquor.

Privately, though, Zimmerman had wondered about the logic of this approach. What the fellow seemed to be saying was that, to do away with crime, all you had to do was make everything legal. His policeman's mind had reacted negatively to that thought. Legal or not, there was something wrong with prostitution, wasn't there? True, you can get rid of the criminal interests by choking off their main sources of money, but, he feared, they always managed to find something else. They were like an octopus—if you cut off one arm, they would only grow another. If you cut off all eight tentacles, he was afraid that eight new ones would regenerate in areas expected the least. According to the papers, they were now into Wall Street, and with the inherent complexities of the stock brokerage business, it sometimes took years before anyone even realized that a crime had been committed. And no doubt, if you got them out of that, they'd pop up somewhere else. It seemed an endless struggle.

He was still pondering these depressing thoughts when he pulled his car into the lot across the street from Brooklyn South.

As soon as he entered the offices of the homicide section, Zimmerman knew that something was wrong. His premonition was confirmed when Lieutenant Snyder, upon seeing him, put down the file he was studying in the anteroom and beckoned him into his office.

Wordlessly, Snyder motioned Zimmerman to sit down while he seated himself behind his desk and stared at his guest for a long moment. Finally, he spoke.

"Al, uh, I hope you weren't planning to hold the funeral today," he began hesitantly. "I know the Jewish tradition and all, but—."

"Why not, Duke?" Zimmerman interrupted. "I thought this was a clear-cut case of an Organization murder? What's the problem?"

"It is, Al. I mean, it still looks like a professional job. But the coroner's office and the captain are insisting on an autopsy. A *full* autopsy."

"What was the matter with the preliminary coroner's examination? My brother had his head half blown off by a gun. Don't tell me there's any doubt as to the cause of death."

"It's not really doubt, Al. It's just that there are a couple of findings in the preliminary examination that don't seem to fit together, that's all."

"What kind of findings?"

By way of answering, Snyder shuffled through the stack of files on his desk, removed one of the thinner folders, and slipped it across to Zimmerman. Zimmerman opened the folder and began reading the first form, a preliminary report from the coroner's office. In so doing, his eyes skimmed the bulk of the report and came to rest on the box labeled "Cause of Death." There he read, "Heart failure due to interruption of the cerebrospinal nervous system, specifically a massive disruption in the medulla oblongata caused by gunshot wound."

He looked up and asked, "So?"

"Al, maybe I'd better show you what's brothering us." Snyder rose and walked to a large movable chalkboard at the side of his office. He quickly erased about a third of the board to give himself room to work. Then he took a piece of chalk and sketched a large oval. "Let's assume that this is the victim's head. Here's the nose, and mouth, and ears, and eyes." As he spoke, he crudely sketched in those features in profile. "Now, the victim was shot through the back of the head, roughly here." He made a chalk mark at the four-o'clock position. "And there were powder burns all over the surrounding skin and hair, indicating that the shot was fired at very close range, perhaps even pressed against the victim's head.

"Here's the peculiar thing, though. The deceased was standing at the head of the stairs when the shot was fired. His heels were no more than six inches from the edge of the top step. The porch there measures only twenty-eight inches between the top step and the sill of the front door, so there isn't too much room for error. Allow that he would have come to the top and reached for the door handle or the bell, and that leaves very little room for anything else. If he had stood at the very edge of the steps, he couldn't have extended his arm to its full length without hitting the door.

"On the basis of this, we could speculate that the killer was standing on a lower step when he fired. Yet, and this is what's throwing us, the bullet traveled in a *downward* path, entering the base of the skull and shattering the medulla and exiting, *not* through the forehead or face, but through the neck. Actually, it smashed from the jaw to the trachea just above the Adam's apple."

He paused and looked over at Zimmerman, who was absorbed in the details.

"Now I don't have to tell you," he continued, "that if the killer was standing beneath the deceased, and the gun was consequently pointed up, the path of the bullet should have been upward, not downward.

"We checked this out with the lab boys, and got them to do some calculations for us. Your brother was five feet eleven inches tall, and he was standing on the top step. If the murderer fired from the step immediately beneath him and was able to compensate for the differential by being taller than your brother, in order to have gotten that angle from the bullet he would've had to be almost eight feet tall. That assumes, of course, that he fired from a normal position holding the gun at, let's say, eye level. Had he reached above his arm level, in stretching to place the gun at the back of the victim's head, the bullet still would have traveled in an upward path, following the angle of his arm.

"In fact, the lab guys tell us that even if the two men were standing on the same level, the path of the bullet would probably have been in a slightly upward angle, as the killer would be lifting the gun to point it. It would have been almost parallel to the ground, but any variation would have been on the side of elevation.

"There are, of course, some possible explanations for the peculiar course the bullet took. If your brother had been looking straight up in the air, with his head tilted back, that might account for it. A complete autopsy should reveal whether that was what happened; the bullet may have creased the front of the top vertebrae. In any event, where it entered the trachea and where it came to rest in the door should tell us whether the trachea was in a stretched position, as it would have been if he was, in fact, looking to the sky.

"We can rule out explaining the downward angle by a sniper or someone on the roof across the street because of the powder burns. Also, I suppose I should tell you, we found the gun right at the scene of the crime."

Zimmerman perked up and raised an eyebrow at Snyder, indicating that he wanted more details. Snyder took the cue and continued.

"It's a nine-millimeter Luger. Typical war souvenir. I don't have to tell you that that means it's just about impossible to trace. We're running a check on the serial number, but I don't think we're that lucky. There must be a hundred thousand guys in this country who brought Lugers home and never bothered to register them. At any rate, one shot had been fired—the rest of the magazine was full. The lab is checking to see if the presence of fresh powder could indicate that more shots were fired and the gun had been reloaded for some reason. They're also doing the standard ballistics analysis to make sure that the gun we found was the murder weapon. That looks pretty positive, though. The killer used old German war-surplus military ammunition, and the slugs in the gun and the one that they removed from the door are of the same type.

"That's another peculiar thing. It isn't like the professional killers we've had experience with to take a chance on ammunition that old. But then, who the hell can predict what those birds will do? It certainly doesn't rule out the murder being an Organization job. It works both ways. Old ammo isn't as reliable, but by the same token it isn't traceable. One thing you can bet on is that we aren't going to find any gun-store clerk who remembers selling the stuff. I'd be willing to bet that the ammo came over in a duffel bag at the same time the gun did. I'm still convinced that it was a professional job. It's just that, frankly, I never saw this wrinkle before."

"Where'd you find the gun?" Zimmerman asked.

"In some bushes alongside the front stairs of the house. No more than six feet from the body, actually. The killer must have dropped it there—probably deliberately dumped it—as soon as he turned to get away."

"Any prints?"

Snyder smiled indulgently. "You've got to be kidding," he replied. "When was the last time you found a murder weapon with fingerprints on it? My God, any kid who reads comic books knows enough to wear gloves or wipe a gun clean so as to not leave any fingerprints. There are some smears on the clip, though. But of course, none of them are clear enough for an identification.

Zimmerman sighed and stared for a moment at Snyder. He could not think of anything else to ask that would put them any closer to finding the killer. Finally he said, "Okay, so you have to do a complete autopsy. When do you think you'll be finished? When can I bury my brother?"

Snyder mustered as sympathetic a look as he could manage. "Al, I told the coroner's office to get it over with as fast as they can. I told them that this was a priority job. They promised me they'd put it at the top of their list."

"That doesn't answer my question. When can I bury my brother?"

"Well, they said they *might* be able to do it today. I suppose you could certainly plan on tomorrow. I'd say you could hold the funeral then, although I'd make it in the afternoon, just to be safe."

"Hmph," Zimmerman snorted as he considered the emotional state the older, more Orthodox members of his family would be in if the funeral couldn't be held today. "Let me ask you this, Duke: Who's the medical examiner on the case? Maybe I could get him to get it done today." He rose to leave.

"Well . . . " Snyder hesitated. "It's Harry Liebowitz over at Coney Island Hospital. But he's a pretty busy guy, Al. Frankly, I think if you try to push him too hard, you might just get the opposite effect. Those fellows are really up to their necks in work, you know."

Zimmerman cast a glance at Snyder as he thought of the two weeks' work that he knew had accumulated on his desk since he went on vacation. "So who isn't?" he replied on his way out.

CHAPTER 8   1706260

THE ANTISEPTIC SMELL of carbolic assaulted Zimmerman's nostrils as he strode toward the reception desk and asked for Dr. Leibowitz. The nurse on duty had to check her lists before she could locate the coroner. She said she knew most of the other staff physicians by sight, but she had very few calls for Leibowitz and doubted if she would recognize him. Upon realizing that Dr. Leibowitz was attached to the coroner's office, she made Zimmerman identify himself before directing him to a subfloor tucked away in the extreme southern corner of the massive medical complex. It took Zimmerman almost ten minutes to find the door labeled "Pathology—County Medical Examiner's Sub-Station."

"Dr. Leibowitz?" Zimmerman called after entering the anteroom and finding it empty. "Is anybody here?"

"Just a minute. Just a minute," an impatient voice answered from one of the three rooms that branched off the small waiting room.

Zimmerman sat down in one of the wooden straight-back chairs that lined the wall and stretched his feet in front of him. For the first time that day, he realized that he was quite tired. He recalled that he had not slept the night before and that he had been running around all day. Fatigue was starting to catch up with him, so he rose and walked to the window. If he stayed in the chair, he was afraid he might doze off, and there was still quite a bit of work to be done.

The door-slamming startled him. "Yeah?" demanded the man who had emerged to the waiting room. "What can I do for you?"

"I'm Al Zimmerman," the policeman began. "Lieutenant Alfred Zimmerman, Manhattan Homicide South. Are you Dr. Leibowitz?"

"Hmph," the doctor grunted by way of an affirmative reply. "Yeah, Zimmerman . . . I remember. Somebody from Brooklyn Homicide called and said you might be by."

He stopped at the reception desk and shuffled through the pile of mail that had been delivered about an hour before. "My secretary is on vacation," he apologized as he ripped open an official-looking letter and read it quickly. He discarded the rest of the mail onto a pile of paper that filled the IN basket and looked up. "What can I do for you, Lieutenant?"

"Two things, really," Zimmerman replied. "First, you've got my brother's body in there. Arnold Zimmerman. Brought in last night, probably. I saw the preliminary report earlier. I'd like to know what else you can tell me about how he died.

"And second, I'd like to know when we can bury him. Our family is Orthodox, you see, and they'll be upset if the funeral has to be postponed past this afternoon. You have to understand how some of the old folks get. . . ."

Dr. Leibowitz raised his hand for Zimmerman to stop. "Lieutenant, I have the same problem at least once a week. Jews always have to be buried in a hurry. I'll tell you the truth, in my line of work, if I weren't Jewish myself, I think I could become anti-Semitic."

The doctor opened a drawer and shuffled through a small sheaf of index cards. "Here we are, Zimmerman, Arnold. Mmhmm. Mmhmm." He looked up at the waiting policeman. Yes. It's okay. The autopsy was completed late this morning. Of course, we're still waiting for some lab tissue and fluid tests to be returned, but I can't see why the body can't be removed and interred whenever you like."

The lieutenant glanced at his watch. One forty. Still plenty of time. "Is it all right if I use your phone to call the undertaker?"

The pathologist nodded and waved his hand at the receiver on the desk. "I'll just go back to work while you're doing that. Give me a holler when you're done."

About twenty minutes later, after he had telephoned the funeral home, the rabbi, his sister-in-law, and his wife, Zimmerman returned the telephone to its cradle for the last time. He paused to rub his burning eyes, then called the doctor.

"Let me ask you something, Lieutenant," Leibowitz began before Zimmerman had a chance to ask any questions, "was your brother a doctor?"

"No," the policeman replied. "Why?"

"Oh, nothing, I guess. It's just that, for some reason, I think I knew him."

"Well, he did go to medical school once, but he didn't make it through. After that, he worked as a medical-supply salesman and as a drug-company detailer for a while. Perhaps you met him that way."

"What medical school?"

"Bellevue."

"Around nineteen fifty sometime?"

"Yes. As a matter of fact, I think it was nineteen fifty-one."

"That's it, then. I was Bellevue, class of fifty-three. I was sure I knew him from somewhere. Too bad. As I recall, he was pretty bright. What happened? Why didn't he finish school? Was it Korea? I remember there were a few guys who left school to enter the war. Was he one of them?"

Zimmerman smiled apologetically. "No such luck or patriotism. He simply flunked out. He was bright enough, all right. He just could never stay at one thing long enough to make a go of it."

The doctor nodded understandingly. "That's a symptom of our times. We instill an image of instant success in our children, and when they see that they have to work hard to achieve anything, they quit. Look at the nineteen-year-old athletes making a hundred thousand dollars a year. Or rock singers not even old enough to grow beards who are making millions.

"Now how do you expect another kid, particularly a bright kid, to accept the fact that he has to work hard and start at the bottom for a few thousand a year . . . and that, at best, he'll be making a comfortable living when he's our age?"

The policeman had a feeling that the pathologist, not having any living patients with whom to converse, was taking advantage of the opportunity to bend his ear. He tried to interrupt in order to get back to the business at hand, but before he could, the doctor was off on another tack.

"No, I can't say I'm surprised when I hear about some kid who can't seem to settle down and work for a living. I hear the same story all the time."

"Oh?" Zimmerman asked patiently.

"Sure, but it's usually from the parents of kids who shot their arms full of crap until it killed them or who jumped out of a window or something. 'He was such a nice boy,' or '. . . such a bright boy. He had everything to live for. Why would he do such a thing?' I'll tell you why the kids do things like that, Lieutenant. Because we never bothered to teach them how to earn their way and to be happy with what they can make for themselves. We always handed them everything on a platter. And then we can't understand why their lives seem purposeless."

The doctor paused and looked into the eyes of the policeman, perceiving that the other was waiting indulgently for him to finish his diatribe.

"You'll have to forgive me, Lieutenant. I get wound up sometimes on this particular subject. I guess I see too much waste that's related to it.

"Now, what else was it that you wanted to know?"

"About my brother's murder, Doctor," Zimmerman said. "What else can you tell me? Lieutenant Snyder indicated that there was something unusual about the angle of the bullet path. Can you give me any more details?"

Liebowitz opened a manila file and shuffled through some papers. "Well, we confirmed the cause of death—the bullet wound at the base of the skull. The bullet did travel an unusual path—downward instead of up—but that could have been caused by a number of things."

"Such as?"

"Well, for one thing, we found that the victim's right wrist and elbow had been strained, very probably quite close to the time of his death. There were signs of strain— the wrist was slightly sprained, in fact—but very little of the discoloration that would normally accompany that type of injury. Possibly the murderer wrenched the victim's arm into a hammerlock just before he shot him. That could account for the head being at an odd angle. Your brother could have been struggling and trying to twist his head around, with an upward cant, when he was shot."

"Anything else?" Zimmerman asked.

The doctor riffled through the pages in the file. "Minor liver damage, probably from drinking, but not of any great magnitude. No, he liked to drink, but he wasn't a drunk. Heart getting a little fatty, but relatively sound. Mmmm, your brother had a duodenal ulcer, you know. No, there really isn't anything else in his physical condition that could tell us anything about why he was murdered or how he died. As I said before, I'm still waiting for the analysis of his stomach contents and the tissue studies, but I rather doubt we'll find anything out of the ordinary there."

"Then you're convinced he was murdered by being shot through the back of the head by a nine-millimeter slug, right?"

"That's right, Lieutenant. I can't see any other way to call it."

Zimmerman thanked the doctor and, after writing down the name of the funeral home that would collect his brother's body and passing the note to Leibowitz so that there could not be any mix-up, he started slowly toward the door. He had been racing around all day and now found that there was nothing else he could do before he went to the funeral, so he walked with no great sense of purpose.

"Mr. Zimmerman," the doctor called after him as he opened the door to leave. He paused and turned to face the doctor. "If it's any comfort, I can tell you that your brother never felt a thing. No pain or anything. As soon as that bullet pierced the medulla oblongata, he was dead. No suffering. He probably never knew what hit him. From that standpoint at least, it was a good way to go."

"Thank you, Doctor," Zimmerman said as he turned and continued on his way out. "Thank you very much."

CHAPTER 9

"I DIDN'T KNOW Arnold Zimmerman very well," the rabbi informed the assembled mourners. "Our paths crossed briefly some thirty-odd years ago when I was an eager, young, newly-ordained rabbi and he was preparing for his bar mitzvah, but that was our most prolonged contact with each other. In the years that have passed since then, I don't think we saw each other more than half a dozen times.

"No, Arnold Zimmerman was not what some of you might consider a religious man. But I spoke today with his loving wife Barbara and his bereaved brother Alfred, and what they told me of his life convinced me that he did not have to come to the synagogue to have lived and died as a good Jew. Arnold Zimmerman may not have followed all the ritual, but he was still a keeper of the Commandments and a man of great faith.

"A rabbi is not really a clergyman, you know. Rather, the term means 'teacher.' And our departed friend must have been a good student, for his faith was not a Sabbath thing, but something he lived.

"Secure in this knowledge, our prayers will not be for him today, but for his family. For his loving wife Barbara, for his son and daughter, Marc and Rebecca, who will no longer have the benefits of his wisdom and guidance, and for all the other friends and relatives in whose hearts Arnold Zimmerman will live forever, let us now join in prayer."

The rabbi began to drone in Hebrew, with the members of the assemblage who knew the words following a half-beat behind.

"V'yisgahdal v'yiskaddash sh'may rabaw . . ."

Up to this point Alfred Zimmerman had tried to maintain a degree of detachment. Listening to the rabbi's words, he had wondered how many times the man had used the same introduction. How many times had he been called upon to bury people he wouldn't have recognized on the street had he met them when they were alive? To some extent, the elder brother found this "to whom it may concern" introduction offensive. His brother had not had a very pleasant life, and it could hardly be said that he set a good example for his children. Rather than having provided guidance for his family, he had always been the weakling and had required their help. But, Zimmerman realized, the rabbi had to say something, and if he had not known his brother very well, that was hardly the rabbi's fault.

It was when the Hebrew prayers started that Zimmerman lost the battle with himself and began to get emotional. The last time he had heard these prayers was when he recited them for his parents. Memories flooded his mind as he mouthed the words by rote.

"Beolomaw b'divraw malchusay . . ."

He felt a pressure on his hand and, glancing down, saw that Kathy was squeezing it tightly. He looked over at her. She was offering him a tissue. His eyes started to ask her why, but then he realized that tears were streaking down his face.

It was not until they were in the limousine, driving to the cemetery, that he began to regain his composure.

CHAPTER 10

"AL, WHAT CAN I say to you?" Sergeant Robert Donofrio offered weakly when Zimmerman entered his office the next day. "We heard about your brother, and the guys asked me to tell you how bad we all feel about it."

"Sure, Bob. Thanks," Zimmerman said as he seated himself behind his desk.

"Some of the guys wanted to send flowers," Donofrio continued, "but Moskowitz said they didn't have flowers at Jewish funerals. Is that right? I mean, we can still send something to your sister-in-law."

Zimmerman nodded affirmatively. "That's right. No flowers. Just send her a condolence card if you want. Forty-two—forty-four East Sixteenth Street, Brooklyn."

"You know, I'm surprised to see you here today. Moskowitz said something about an official period of mourning. Shiva, I think he called it."

"Yeah. I sent Kathy over there this morning to see if there was anything she could do. Help take care of the kids, or something. Me, I'd go crazy sitting there with nothing to do but feel bad."

The lieutenant picked up an eight-inch-thick pile of papers that rested in his IN basket. "I've got to keep busy, Bob. You know me."

"That's the same way I'd feel," the sergeant agreed. "By the way, did Snyder have any leads on the murderer? I've got some friends over at Brooklyn South if you need a pipeline."

Zimmerman sighed. "I talked to Duke yesterday, Bob. The way they figure it, it was a professional job and we've got about as much chance as the proverbial snowball in hell of ever apprehending anybody for it."

Zimmerman paused meaningfully. "You know, logically, I can look at the facts and I have to come to much the same conclusion. If it were my case, I'd feel the way Snyder does —that it would be a waste of time and manpower to pursue it. I mean, look at the circumstances—my brother was a habitual gambler, he was in to the bookies for some money which, if I knew him the way I think I did, he simply didn't have, and he ends up murdered very conspicuously on his own doorstep. It has all the earmarks of a professional assassination. We've seen it happen before, and we all know that the chances of ever catching the killer are practically nil. I was thinking about it last night, and the only case of this kind that I can remember we solved in the past ten years was that bookmaker on the Lower East Side who got killed for holding out on his bosses. And the only reason we got a break in that case was that one of our informers cracked during one of those "family" power struggles three years later. Three years, for God's sake! We didn't really solve that murder; the solution was handed to us as a gift.

"So I don't know what the chances would be here. Pretty poor, at best." Zimmerman looked at his sergeant friend for a moment. "I can accept all that on a professional level. What's the expression Dr. Collier uses—I can intellectualize it. But in here"—he brought his clenched fist to his solar plexus—"all I want to do is catch the son of a bitch who murdered my brother!"

Donofrio nodded, indicating that he understood the feeling and sympathized. "Well, Snyder will do everything he can, Al. In the meantime, if you want, I'll get hold of a guy I know over in Brooklyn South who owes me a few favors. If there are any breaks in the case, he can keep us informed."

"No, Bob. Don't. Snyder promised me he'd let me know if anything changed, and I wouldn't want him to think I was going behind his back. You save those favors for when you really need something in return.

"Right now"—Zimmerman hefted the pile of paperwork that had accumulated during his vacation—"it looks as if I've got work to do."

The sergeant turned to leave the office.

"Oh, Bob . . ." Zimmerman called after him. He turned. "Bob, thanks for listening. I had to get that off my chest."

Donofrio smiled and resumed his journey back to his own desk.

The stack of paper had been reduced by only about an inch and a half when the phone rang Lieutenant Zimmerman out of his deep concentration. Most of the paperwork had been of a routine nature, but as the administrative head of his unit, Zimmerman dared not allow any of it to escape his scrutiny. 'More careers have been ended by guys signing things they hadn't fully read or understood than from other single cause' was a piece of advice that had been given Zimmerman when he first assumed his lieutenancy, and he had not found any reason to doubt it. Indeed, it was by monitoring the paper flow that Zimmerman had learned that he could keep his department functioning efficiently without injecting himself in every minor situation.

Even so, the work had a tendency to get dull, and it was only the fact that he was concentrating deliberately in order to close his mind to the other events transpiring around him that enabled him to lose himself in it.

Instinctively, without removing his eyes from the document he was reading, he lifted the receiver.

"Homicide, Lieutenant Zimmerman speaking."

"Al? Kathy. Have you got a minute?" his wife replied.

"I'm pretty busy, Kath. What's the matter?"

"I'm still in Brooklyn, Al, with Barbara and the kids. Do you know anything about Arnie's insurance?"

"No. Why?"

"Well, it's a long story and it looks pretty complicated. Could you come over here this evening when you're finished working, perhaps?"

"I don't know when that'll be, Kath. You know what the first day back is like. I've got enough reports on my desk to paper the walls of Penn Station. Can't it wait a couple of days?"

"I don't think so. Barbara's upset about it."

"I thought she was supposed to be in mourning. Why is she worrying about insurance companies now?"

"Well, it wasn't her idea, believe me. A man showed up here a little while ago from the insurance company. He just left. Look, he left some forms to sign that I think you ought to take a look at. Can you get away at lunch time, maybe?"

"Kathy," Zimmerman said in an exasperated tone, "it takes three quarters of an hour to get there from here and three quarters of an hour back. I can take an hour for lunch when I'm *not* too busy. Right now I'm up to my ears in work."

"Well," his wife paused, "Maybe we can do it over the phone. . . ."

"Oh, all right," Zimmerman finally gave in, "but I can't see why she doesn't just get herself a lawyer. I'm only a cop, you know."

His wife ignored this advice and began: "Well, as I said, a little while ago an insurance man showed up here and he handed Barbara a check for eleven thousand dollars and change that he said represented payment on Arnie's life insurance policy. He seemed nice enough, and expressed his condolences and all that, but Barbara got upset with the amount. She insisted that Arnie had at least a hundred thousand dollars in life insurance. Naturally enough, she wanted to know what this eleven thousand represented. So the insurance man said that it was payment in full on the policy with his company and he handed her some kind of disclaimer that, the way I read it, said if she accepted the check it was all she was going to get from them, ever. Well, Barbara told him that she'd have to think about it and asked him to leave the paper for her to look over. Then he started getting a little pushy. He told her that his company prided itself on settling claims right away and she should consider herself lucky that they wanted to settle so quickly. Well, that's when I stepped in and told him that he was upsetting Barbara and that he should leave the forms. We'd be getting back to him within the next few days. He didn't seem to like that idea very much, but he did as I asked. I really think you should look at them, Al."

"Maybe Arnie had policies with other companies, too." Zimmerman said. "Does Barbara know where he kept his important papers? Don't they have a safe deposit box or something?"

"She's looking now. I asked her the same question, and she said they didn't have a safe deposit box. Arnie kept everything in a desk drawer."

"That figures," Zimmerman acknowledged, recognizing that that would have been in keeping with the way his brother did things.

"Wait a minute. Here she comes now."

There was a long pause during which the policeman heard only the sound of paper rustling. He drummed his fingers restlessly on his desk, glancing over at the stack of reports

47

that still awaited his attention. Just as he picked up the top sheet and began to read it again, his wife returned to the phone.

"This is crazy, Al. It's the same insurance company, all right. Champlain Insurance Company. But this policy definitely says one hundred thousand dollars. It's typed in, right on the first page.

"I knew that eleven-thousand-plus figure was screwy. I never heard of an insurance policy written in an odd amount like that. It's always ten thousand, or twenty thousand, or a hundred thousand or something, isn't it? It's always a round number. I never heard of one that wasn't."

Zimmerman thought for a moment. He then asked, "Do you know if Arnie had borrowed against it? That could reduce the amount to something odd like that. And he always needed money."

"I don't know, Al. I wish you could take a look at these papers, though."

"All right, Kath. I'll tell you what—bring them home with you tonight and I'll go over them. But I still think Barbara would do a lot better with a lawyer. After all, they're paid to know their way around these things. If she doesn't know any, I'm sure I could ask around the office and find somebody for her."

"I suggested that, too, Al." Her voice grew conspiratorial. "But I think what it comes down to is that you do know something about the law and you're a heck of a lot cheaper."

"Yeah," the lieutenant admitted. "You can't get any cheaper than free."

Before he left for home that night, Zimmerman placed a call to his counterpart in Brooklyn. As he had expected, there were no earthshaking developments to report. That a handkerchief found in the bushes near the body had been identified by the laundry mark as belonging to his brother

48

was the only new data.

My wife washes my hankies, he thought as he drove home. I can't afford to send them out. Immediately, he chided himself for the thought. This was no time to become irritated anew about his brother's wasteful ways.

CHAPTER 11

"HELLO, MRS. ZIMMERMAN?" the man's voice on the phone asked.

"Yes?" the lieutenant's wife replied, still at the home of her sister-in-law.

"Mrs. Zimmerman, first I want to express our sympathy at the loss of your husband."

"Oh, wait a minute. I think you want to talk to—"

"But you know, Mrs. Zimmerman," the voice interrupted, "he did owe us quite a lot of money. Over two thousand dollars, in fact."

"But I'm not the Mrs. Zimmerman you want—"

"We want our money, Mrs. Zimmerman. That's what we want."

"Who is this?"

"That's not important. All you have to know is that before he died, Mr. Zimmerman was in to us for, uh, two thousand one hundred and fifty-four dollars. Now we appreciate the position you're in, Mrs. Zimmerman, and we're sorry about your loss. But business is business. We want our money as soon as possible."

"But if I don't even know who you are, how do I know he really owed you this money?"

"He owed it to us, Mrs. Zimmerman. You can take my word for it. And I'd advise you very strongly to believe me. To do otherwise could have some very unpleasant side effects."

50

"But—"

"No buts, Mrs. Zimmerman. Two thousand one hundred and fifty-four dollars. I'll tell you what. We're willing to be nice about it. We'll call it two thousand dollars even, and accept a small loss. Now, can you have it for us within two weeks? You should have some insurance money by then."

"I don't think so. You see, we're arguing with the insurance company about the amount. It might take quite a while."

"I'm afraid you're wrong about that, Mrs. Zimmerman. It can't take quite a while. It can't take more than two weeks, in fact. That's our deadline. Two thousand dollars by two weeks from today."

Kathy's voice grew hoarse. Even though the thinly-veiled threats were not directed at her, she was frightened.

"How will I get it to you? God, I don't even know who you are. How can I pay you when I don't even know your name or where to reach you?"

"Don't worry about that, Mrs. Zimmerman. We'll contact you. Two weeks from today. And you'd better have the money for us. No checks, either. Cash on the line. Two thousand dollars."

Kathy Zimmerman stood dumbfounded, holding the receiver to her ear even after she had heard the click. She didn't replace the instrument in its cradle until she was brought back to reality by the sound of the dial tone. Slowly, she sank into the chair beside the telephone table and began to put together her thoughts concerning the call.

"Who was that, Kathy?" Barbara Zimmerman asked as she entered the room.

"I don't know. He wouldn't leave a name."

She rose from the chair and went to her sister-in-law, placing her arm over her shoulder consolingly. "It was really for you. Something about a lot of money that Arnie owed somebody." Barbara Zimmerman looked up at her for further explanation.

"Do you know anything about Arnie having borrowed two thousand dollars from anybody?" Kathy asked.

Barbara nodded her head from side to side dumbly. Then she said, "No. I know Arnie was always in hock and never had any money, but I certainly don't know anything about any two thousand dollars. To tell you the truth, I don't even know who would lend him that kind of money. I mean, I loved Arnie very much, don't misunderstand me, but I knew his weaknesses. And let's face it, anybody who would loan Arnie that kind of money would have to be crazy. My late husband's credit rating was not exactly A-One, you know."

"Ummm," Kathy mumbled by way of a noncommittal reply as she recalled the house that she and Al had planned on buying until Al had had to use the down payment money to get his brother out of some scrape a few years back. "In all those papers in the desk, was there a loan agreement or anything like that?"

"Not that I could tell. Of course, I don't know what half those things are."

"All right," Kathy said. "Look, give me all those papers and I'll take them home with me tonight. Maybe Al will be able to figure them out. In the meantime, don't worry about it. We'll work something out." She gave her sister-in-law's arm a reassuring squeeze and started looking for her sweater.

On her way home on the subway, Kathy Zimmerman could not help but think, as she looked at the name of the chic shop emblazoned on the shopping bag in which she carried the jumble of documents, that for all her in-laws' actual state of poverty, they managed to shop in better stores than she could.

CHAPTER 12

"I DON'T GET IT," Zimmerman complained to Sergeant Donofrio as they rode up in the elevator the next morning. "I've just never heard of anything like it before."

The two men strode off the elevator and entered the lieutenant's office without pausing to acknowledge the presence of other detectives who sat at their desks in the outer office. Donofrio seated himself in one of the leather-cushioned wooden chairs opposite the desk while Zimmerman went to the window and stared out dramatically.

Suddenly he turned and faced the sergeant. "I've been dealing with criminals all my adult life. I've had my share of experience with organized crime, too. But I never heard of them first killing somebody and then trying to collect on the dead man's debts! It doesn't make any sense, Bob."

"Al," the sergeant said, when his superior finally finished his tirade, "do you remember what you once told me a few years ago about this being the age of the bookkeeper? You were particularly annoyed, as I recall, about the paperwork jungle and filling out forms in triplicate just so some clerks could be kept busy. You said that it really didn't matter what anybody did anymore, just so long as it was properly documented. Do you remember that?"

The angry lieutenant nodded that he did recall the incident.

"Well," the sergeant offered, "maybe the Mafia finally started recruiting at Harvard Business School. The guy saw that the books didn't balance, so he decided to turn the matter over to "Accounts Receivable" for collection. You know how the *legitimate* collection agencies work. As long as they think there's a chance of getting paid, they keep trying. Remember, when the Organization killed your brother, they did it as a warning to other people who owed them money—not as a means of collecting what *he* owed them. They probably figure that the widow will pay. After all, her husband's just been murdered, so she's already scared. It's extortion in a way, but I'm sure they view it as simply collecting a debt."

The lieutenant listened patiently until his friend had finished.

"I wonder . . ." he began. "Is that really the way the hoods are working now? Or . . ."

"Or what?"

"Or is it possible that the Mafia or the Organization or the Cosa Nostra or the Syndicate or whatever the hell they're called this week didn't have anything to do with my brother's death and they're trying to take advantage of an existing situation?"

"I don't follow."

"Look: Let's just say say that you are a bookie or a loan shark. You've got a guy in to you for a couple of thousand and he gets himself murdered. It looks like an Organization job, so you get sore because you didn't have anything to do with it. The first thing you do is pick up a phone and call your own superior and complain. He checks around—it wouldn't take long—and calls you back and tells you that the Organization didn't set it up and doesn't know anything about it. Now, you're still pretty small potatoes, so you believe him because you don't really have any choice. You're a smart cop. What conclusions does that leave open to you?"

"That somebody else murdered your brother?"

"Who?"

"Uh, how should I know? It could have been almost anybody."

"Come on now. Who commits most of the murders we handle?"

"Husbands murder their wives."

"Right! And wives murder their husbands!"

The sergeant was shocked. He began hesitantly: "Al, are you really suggesting that your sister-in-law . . . ?"

"No. Or at least I don't think so. But I am saying that that's what the bookmaker or loan shark who made that phone call might have thought. I don't know what really happened any more than you do, but this is the first good thing that's happened yet."

"Good?"

"Sure. Dissension in the ranks and all that. Look, in all likelihood, my brother was murdered by the Organization, exactly as Snyder suspects. But for some reason, they didn't bother to tell the member of their family to whom he owed the money. Why, I don't know. But they kept one of their boys in the dark. At least that's a place to start, isn't it?"

"How can *that* help us? I mean, okay, maybe there's a "family" feud in the offing. But I still can't see how it does us any good. Unless you are figuring that maybe somebody will come forward and finger someone else."

"Well, that could happen, I suppose. But that's not what I'm counting on at all. I'm going to use that money as a lever to get inside the Organization and see what's going on."

"You're going to pay the money?"

"Of course. How else can I find out who wants it?"

CHAPTER 13

BARNEY FINKLE was not exactly a friend of Al Zimmerman—Finkle really didn't have any friends that he had met in the course of his work—but he was a competent lawyer. A short man with a substantial paunch, he modeled his attire and moustache after Adolph Menjou, whom he thought he resembled. Somehow, though, he had never achieved the actor's elegance. Instead, a sharp glint in his eyes gave him an air of cunning that forespoke any hint of aristocratic bearing. He was not at his best in a courtroom—juries tended to distrust him. But in the closed conference rooms of a corporation or insurance company with which he was engaged in combat, his appearance alone let his adversaries know that they were dealing with a man who knew his business.

In the trade, he was sometimes referred to with a degree of grudging admiration as "Barney the Settler." He was always willing to settle a case out of court, albeit at *his* price. Although such matters were kept in the strictest confidence, it had become known that Finkle had been able to achieve settlements that seemed inordinately large. Knowing Finkle's reputation, Zimmerman decided that he was the attorney best able to handle his brother's estate—particularly the negotiations with the insurance company.

"This is going to cost you," the lawyer declared after he had finished perusing the pile of papers that the lieutenant had deposited on his mahogany desk. "Do you know how I work?"

"Not really," Zimmerman answered defensively.

"I don't take a retainer," the lawyer explained. "I work on a contingency basis. A percentage of the total. I get twenty-five percent of the final settlement. And that's cheap. Some of my esteemed colleagues want fifty."

Zimmerman looked a little surprised at the magnitude of the fee, and expressed this. "That's a lot of money, though. This is a hundred-thousand-dollar policy, so that means your fee would be twenty-five thousand dollars."

The lawyer smiled indulgently and launched forth into an explanation he had given so often he repeated it by rote.

"In the first place, Mr. Zimmerman, as I said, if I lose, I get nothing. And at the risk of shaking your confidence in me, I must admit that I have lost a few cases in the course of my career. The insurance company obviously does not want to part with the money, and it's going to take a lot of work and time on my part to get them to live up to their obligation. I'm not going to say that I'm not well paid, but believe me, I earn my money. Besides, you have to look at it as twenty-five percent of something that doesn't exist now. They offered you only eleven thousand, remember. You're still free to accept that offer, you know. But if, let's say, I can get you eighty thousand—even after I take my twenty, you've still got sixty. You're way ahead of the game."

"There's a point here I must be missing," Zimmerman interjected with some consternation. "My brother had a life insurance policy with a face value of one hundred thousand dollars. My brother died. Why doesn't the insurance company pay the hundred thousand? Why is it necessary to go through all this just to get them to honor their contract? It is a contract, isn't it?"

The lawyer's face took on the same expression as that of a father explaining to a little boy that hard-boiled eggs can't hatch, even if you do put them on the electric blanket.

"Lieutenant," he answered, "your naïveté surprises me. I

would have expected a police officer to know a little more about human nature than that.

"Insurance companies are profit-making enterprises. Very substantial profits at that. They like to keep it that way. There are even some companies who will try to save money by *not* paying the full value of claims against them whenever they think they can get away with it. You must remember that, to a great extent, the rates charged by insurance companies are set by law. The maximums are, at least. These laws allow for a reasonable profit, but that's not good enough for some insurance guys. Their view is that if they can chisel ten, twenty, thirty percent off each claim, they're increasing their profits. And that, they'll argue, is only good business. Now, sometimes they pay the full amount straightaway. But that's usually on the five- and ten-thousand-dollar policies. Although I've seen them get tricky on those, too. When they *do* pay the full amount quickly, it usually means that they simply can't see any way around it.

"Okay; so much for history and the big picture. Let's take a look at your case."

"Wait a minute. Wait a minute. Let me make sure I understand this. You're telling me that the insurance companies deliberately try to cheat their beneficiaries? But they have a contract! If the policy is for a hundred thousand dollars, say, and they only want to pay fifty, why can't someone just sue them?"

"Oh, they can. And sometimes they do. But let me ask you a question—you have a lot of dealings with the criminal courts; how long do your cases have to wait on the calendar before they come to trial?"

"Usually something between twelve and eighteen months."

"Twelve to eighteen months," the lawyer repeated. "Well, in the civil courts it often takes five or six years before a case is heard. Five or six years.

"Just assume for the moment that you're a widow in your

58

sister-in-law's position. You have no other source of income, right? Can you afford to go without anything for five or six years? No, of course not. So at some point you're going to get tired of waiting and you're going to take what they give you.

"But look, don't get me wrong. There are still many outfits that don't do business this way; companies that pay promptly and in full. Frankly, it's just your bad luck that your brother didn't insure his life with one of them. This outfit"—he picked up the policy and dropped it back on his desk for effect—"I've dealt with before. They're not exactly Santa Claus, believe me."

The policeman sat in his chair, unable to speak. He had never realized that the insurance companies, who set up an image of themselves as public benefactors, would really do business in this unethical fashion.

"Why this case?" he finally asked. "You said that even this company pays promptly some of the time. What made them choose this particular case to get cheap about? And how, by the way, did they ever come up with such an odd figure—eleven thousand one hundred and twenty-eight dollars?"

"I'll answer your second question first. They arrived at the amount pretty much by chance. What probably happened was that two or three of their people sat around and wrote down amounts they thought would make a good first offer. Then they averaged them. Now that may not seem to make a great deal of sense, but from their vantage point it does. But that still might not give you such an unusual number. No, they do that very deliberately so that the person receiving the check will think that they figured it out to the penny. Look at it another way: If you are selling a car to me and I ask you what you want for it and you say five hundred dollars, then I know it's only an asking price. If you tell me that the price is five hundred and twenty dollars, then I'm going to be much less likely to dicker. I am going to assume that you must have reached that price by some kind of figuring, and that the price is firm. It works. Try it next time you've got a car to sell.

"So the amount of their first offer is pretty arbitrary. They expect to have to negotiate, but, like all businessmen, they'd prefer not to. You following me?"

The policeman nodded with interest.

"Okay, now for your other question. Why did they pick this case to get tough about?

"Well, the primary reason is that they do have a leg to stand on here."

"Huh?" Zimmerman asked.

The attorney held up his hand to indicate that his audience should give him a chance to finish what he was saying.

"What I mean by that is that they can stall legitimately. If, let's say, your brother had died as a result of a coronary —a natural death, if you will—they would be a lot easier to do business with. Just for your information, they would have had a different first offer, then. Based on my experience, what they usually do in cases of large amounts of insurance money due the beneficiary in a natural death, is to offer an annuity in lieu of a lump sum. Talk about con artists! And I've seen more people than you'd believe who fell for it. What they do is tell the grieving widow that instead of paying her a hundred thousand dollars all at once, they'll do her a favor and pay her a hundred dollars a week for something like twenty years.

"And all that time, while they're doing her this big favor and sending her weekly checks, they're drawing at least eight percent interest on the hundred thousand. She could have taken the money, put it in a savings bank, and drawn an income—and she'd still have the principle, the hundred thousand. It wouldn't be for just twenty years, either.

60

"But they can be very convincing when they're dealing with an emotionally upset woman, as any recent widow is bound to be. Before she knows it, they've talked her into this ploy of theirs and she's signed the paper."

"Okay. Enough digressing. Let's talk about what's happening in your case. As I indicated, your brother did not die a natural death. In point of fact, he was murdered. That's all they need to hold up a settlement practically forever. Or at least until the murderer is found and convicted. You probably know as well as I do that under the law, a felon cannot legally profit by his crime. If you murdered your wife, and it could be proved and you were convicted, you would cease to be an heir at law."

"Are they contending that my sister-in-law murdered my brother?"

"Not at all. They're much too sharp to actually make any accusations of that sort. But as long as that continues to be a possibility, they can withhold any payment. And if you sought any kind of punitive damages for their stalling tactics, they could go right into court and argue that they're waiting for the crime to be solved. The judge would grant them all the delays they wanted, too."

Zimmerman sat in thoughtful silence as he digested what the attorney had told him. When he spoke, there was a note of helplessness in his voice. "They've really got us where they want us, don't they? I mean, everything seems to be in their favor. No matter where the right and wrong of the situation lies, they get their way. I never would have dreamed that any insurance companies operated like that. Isn't there anything we can do?"

"Well, as I said before, most insurance companies don't work this way. In all fairness, I'd have to say that the majority are aboveboard. But this one, the Champlain . . ." He paused for effect, then shifted gears. "To answer your real question, though—yes, there are things that we can do. But

61

I'm going to need your help.

"The first thing that has to be done is to have me put officially on this case. Now, you told me on the phone before you came over that you are not a beneficiary in this estate—your sister-in-law is. Well, she will have to retain me before I can really go to work. Of course, if she wants another lawyer, she's welcome to choose her own, but I cannot advise too strongly that she gets someone. By the way, in the event that I'm not retained, you'll be getting a bill from me for this session now." He pointed to the quotation from Abraham Lincoln that was framed and mounted on his wall: A lawyer's time and advice are his stock in trade. "Probably fifty bucks. Okay?"

Zimmerman nodded in agreement.

"Assuming that your sister-in-law retains me, I'll need your help. As I see it at this point, my first course of action would be to get a show-cause order against the Champlain, which demands that they either pay the full amount or else 'show cause' why they shouldn't. Now that should wake them up and let them know that they're not just dealing with a bewildered widow. Also, it can be done fairly quickly. We could probably get a hearing on that within a couple of months. But the thing I'll need from you is a statement from the police department, more specifically from the officer in charge of investigating your brother's murder, that your sister-in-law is not a suspect. Do you think you could get a statement like that for me?"

"I don't know," Zimmerman answered. "I spoke to the lieutenant who heads Brooklyn South Homicide and he told me that they strongly suspect that it was a Mafia-kind of murder. In fact, that's the only theory they're operating on right now. Frankly, looking at the case objectively—the manner of the crime and the lack of tangible evidence or any motive—I'd have to agree that that's the best bet. The trouble with that, though, is that it means in all likelihood

62

the actual murderer will never be caught. Obviously, the best way to prove that my sister-in-law didn't do it would be to prove that someone else did. And that's going to be hard, if not impossible.

"Whether Lieutenant Snyder in Brooklyn would be willing to go into court and testify that they have definitely eliminated my brother's wife as a suspect, I just don't know. I mean I think I could probably get him to stand up and say that she certainly isn't a prime suspect, but I've seen you lawyers in operation—if he were asked whether she had been absolutely, definitely, positively eliminated; if the question were phrased, 'Are you positive that Mrs. Zimmerman did not kill her husband?', he'd probably have to concede that there was a vague possibility that she had done it. Would that be enough to allow the insurance company to withhold payment?"

"Could be," the lawyer answered. "It depends on the judge. And you can bet that even if the first judge ruled in our favor, some appeals court would probably reverse him. It would be worth a try, though. If for no other reason than to let Champlain know that we're not going to take this lying down. It would certainly give us a better position from which to negotiate. Let's see, we can get this Snyder guy to testify, and the next-door neighbor and the investigating officers. They can state that she was hysterical from grief. She doesn't have a psychiatrist, does she?"

Zimmerman raised his hands, palms up, to indicate that he didn't know.

"I guess it would be too much to hope for that she had an analyst who would testify that he had known her for a long time and that such things as murder didn't fit her psychological makeup. That's wishful thinking on my part, I suppose.

"At any rate, we'll need some witnesses to demonstrate that she has no other income and that to deprive her of her rightful insurance money represents cruel and unusual punishment." The attorney was thinking out loud now. "I don't know. Maybe we do have a case here. We always have our secret weapon, of course."

"Secret weapon?"

"The newspapers. I don't know how you or your sister-in-law feel about publicity like that, but if we can get the papers interested in the case, that might be just the lever we need. Picture a story in the newspapers: 'Widow on Welfare Denied Insurance Money,' with a full description of just how crooked Champlain really is. I can give them some pretty good quotes myself. Things like 'I've had this experience with Champlain before. They'll do everything they can to avoid paying on legitimate claims.'

"Nobody needs that kind of publicity, but particularly an insurance company that wants to find new suckers and sell new policies. Hell, we might even be able to get the story on the six-o'clock news on television."

"I don't know whether my sister-in-law would be willing to make a public spectacle of herself," Zimmerman said. "I suppose we could ask her."

"Well, don't bother at this point. That's a last resort, after all. Champlain hasn't really kept her on the string long enough to make it a valid story anyway. You need at least a year of stalling before the newspapers will really think it's newsworthy. We've got plenty of time for that later.

"The thing to do now," said the lawyer as he rose from his seat and walked around to escort Zimmerman to the door, "is for you to fill your sister-in-law in on what we discussed this afternoon and get her to retain me. I can't do anything until she does that. If she wants to discuss it with me herself, I'll be happy to give her an appointment. Just give me a call, okay?"

Zimmerman joined Finkle at the office door. "Sure. Either way, I'll call you within the next few days."

The warm, mild air bathed Lieutenant Zimmerman when he stepped out into the street, refreshing him. Glancing at his watch, he saw that it was just two o'clock, so he started walking the seven blocks back to his office rather than taking a bus. For the first time since his return from vacation he felt that he was beginning to fit back into his old groove. He consciously tried to slow his step to a stroll as he headed back. But before he had gone a block, he had been caught up in the fast pace of the crowd that had been passing him, and he was hurrying along the sidewalk as if he were late for an appointment. By the time he reached the Manhattan South headquarters building, he was perspiring freely.

"Rank has its privileges," he thought as he entered the office of his captain, in response to a note he had found waiting on his desk. The captain's suite was one of the few offices in the building that boasted air-conditioning. The cool draft reminded him of how sweaty he was, yet did little to make him feel more comfortable.

"Yes, sir?" Zimmerman asked as he confronted his superior officer.

"Oh, hello, Al," Captain Cornelius McIlhenny greeted him in a stilted attempt at informality. "Sit down, sit down, please." McIlhenny had been at Manhattan South for slightly more than a year. He had come downtown from Bronx Homicide to replace Captain O'Brien, who had been Zimmerman's boss for eleven years. It had only been in the past couple months that McIlhenny had shown any signs of becoming comfortable in his captaincy and with the men in his new command.

Zimmerman seated himself and looked at McIlhenny expectantly.

"Uh, Al, let me ask you, uh, how are you feeling?"

"Fine, sir. Why do you ask?"

"Oh, no reason, Al. It's just that a loss in the family, particularly a close loss, affects different people in different ways. You know, if you don't feel like . . . uh, I should say, uh, if you feel like taking some time off, I checked and you've got plenty of sick time coming. I'd certainly okay a request for a week of it now."

"Mac," Zimmerman began familiarly, "I just got back from vacation. I've got a ton of work waiting for me. I can't take any more time off now. I do appreciate the offer, though."

Zimmerman rose to leave.

"Wait a minute, Al," McIlhenny interrupted, rejecting Zimmerman's attempt at affability. "I want to talk to you."

Zimmerman reseated himself.

"This is very difficult, Al. We've known each other for a long time and I've got a great deal of respect for you, both as a man and as a cop. I can understand what you're going through as a man, but as a cop, as a professional policeman, I've got to warn you about something. You can't let the two things get mixed up."

Zimmerman looked quizzically at the captain, not understanding.

"Maybe I'm not making myself very clear, Al. What I'm trying to tell you is that you can't allow the fact that you're a normal man with normal feelings and that your brother was just murdered influence your judgment as a policeman. What I'm trying to say is that I can appreciate what you're going through, but let Brooklyn South worry about catching the killer."

Zimmerman became defensive. "I don't think I understand you, Captain. Are you trying to tell me that I've been getting in Snyder's way?"

"No, Al. I didn't say that. I'm just warning, no . . . cautioning, you not to. Snyder's a good cop, too. And a very thorough one. He knows his business and if anybody can find your brother's killer, he can. All I'm asking is that you let him do his job."

"*If* anybody can find the killer? Then you don't think it can be done either?"

"Well, I did discuss the case with Snyder, of course, and you have to admit the chances don't look too good. But believe me, Al, and if you were thinking more clearly, you'd see this yourself—Snyder will do the best job he can. He hasn't simply filed the case, if that's what you think. They're still investigating. I spoke to him just this morning."

"Anything new?"

"No."

Lieutenant Zimmerman studied his superior's face thoughtfully, then asked, "Captain, let me ask you—what brought all this on? Okay, I went over to Brooklyn South and I looked at their file on the case. In fact, Snyder offered it to me. I hardly had to ask for it. But that's really all I've done. You make it sound as if I'm trying to be a one-man police force, and I don't think I've done anything to justify that conclusion."

"Al, Donofrio told me about the phone call and your plans to pay the money and see where it leads."

Zimmerman was shocked. What he had discussed with his friend had, he thought, been in confidence.

"Don't blame him, Al. He was only trying to protect you when he came and told me. He saw what you're being too bullheaded to see for yourself—that you could get yourself killed playing these games. You're not Sam Spade, you know."

Zimmerman's mouth took on lines of anger as he spoke. "Captain, there's something about this whole thing that bothers me. And it has very little to do with the fact that the victim was my brother. As soon as anybody around here mentions organized crime, it looks as if we all put our tails between our legs and run scared. All right, I'll grant you that I used to do the same thing—not run scared, but I'd just shelve the cases that had a professional look about them because I know as well as anybody in Homicide that the chances of solving them are less. But for God's sake," he pleaded, "that doesn't mean they can't be solved. I know that it's more efficient to spend our limited time and resources on cases where we stand a better chance of success. I can appreciate Snyder's position because I've done the same thing myself. But maybe the fact that it was my brother in this case has given me a different perspective.

"You know what it reminds me of? During the First World War, the generals used to sit around and carefully calculate the losses they would sustain before each battle. And they used to say things like 'Well, we're going to have forty percent of our soldiers killed if we charge this ridge. We can afford that, so let's do it.' They never thought of their troops as people who didn't particularly want to be sacrificed.

"We're doing the same thing. We sit around and say, 'Well, we solved twenty-six cases this month. That's up from twenty three last month, so we must be doing better.' And we don't give one good goddamn for the cases we write off as unsolvable unless we're lucky. We look at our solution rates and as long as the line on the graph keeps going up, we act satisfied. If a case looks too rough for us, or looks as if it might require a lot of work, we start hunting for angles to get rid of it. Is it interstate? Good, then we can turn it over to the FBI. Did the guy live in Westchester? Maybe we can get the State Police to take it over. Does it look like a professional job? Well, then, we know those are tough, so let's just stick it in a file with a lot of others and see if there's a pattern. We've got more excuses!"

Zimmerman, his tirade having ended, slumped in the chair. He continued to glower at the captain accusingly.

"Are you finished?" McIlhenny inquired, choking on his own temper.

Zimmerman did not speak.

"You said something about having a ton of work to catch up with. I suggest you either do it or take me up on my offer for sick time. Dismissed!"

"Thanks, pal," Zimmerman said sarcastically as he passed Sergeant Donofrio's desk on the way back to his own office. "Thanks a lot!"

"Why, what's the matter?" Donofrio asked with a degree of injured innocence.

"I just got my tail chewed by McIlhenny, that's what's the matter. Because you couldn't keep your mouth shut."

Donofrio followed Zimmerman into his office. "I did it for your own good, Al," the sergeant said defensively.

The lieutenant glared. "Do me a favor, will you? Let me be the judge of what's for my own good and what isn't. You know, when I discuss something like my brother's death with you, I would think you would know that what I'm saying is just between the two of us. I don't expect you to go around broadcasting my personal business to anybody who might listen."

"That's not fair, Al. I just didn't want to see you get yourself hurt playing around with organized crime, that's all. They don't play by the rules, at least not any set of rules that we'd approve of. Believe me, they'd just as soon kill you as not."

"Oh, I see," Zimmerman said even more sarcastically, "If there's any danger involved, we're supposed to forget about it. What the hell kind of cop are you, anyway? Why do you think the Department issued us guns? So that we could avoid exposing ourselves to any possible danger?"

"To protect ourselves from danger, yes. To take foolish, unnecessary risks, no. And for you to investigate this crime on your own by trying to worm your way into the inner circles of organized crime is taking unnecessary risks, as far as I'm concerned."

"As far as *you're* concerned? Last time I looked, I was the lieutenant and you were still the sergeant. What the hell gives you the right to make decisions like that? Who are you to be concerned?"

"I'm your friend, Al, in case you've forgotten. That gives me the right to be concerned. And if you weren't bound and determined to be so obstinate, you'd see that what I did was for your own good."

Zimmerman stared belligerently at Donofrio, recognizing that there was truth in what he said, yet reluctant to admit his friend's good intentions.

"By the way, Al," Donofrio said as he get up to leave, "are we having dinner together tonight?" The Zimmerman and Donofrio families had a long-standing commitment to share meals on Thursday nights—one week at Zimmerman's home, the next week at Donofrio's.

"I don't think so, Bob," Zimmerman replied, his voice calmer now. "Things are still pretty hectic. You understand."

"Sure."

Donofrio stepped toward the door as Zimmerman looked at the pile of paperwork on his desk. The stack had again risen to eight inches.

CHAPTER 14

"What a day!" Al Zimmerman declared as he paused at his hall closet to hang up his jacket. Automatically, he removed his gun harness and, folding the straps as he walked, carried the weapon and its rigging into the bedroom, where he locked them in the tin box on his closet shelf.

"What a goddamn brutal day!"

"Busy?" his wife inquired when he joined her in the kitchen and seated himself at the dinette table.

"Aah, not just that. Just one of those days when everything went wrong and nothing went right. First I went to see a lawyer about Arnie's insurance, and he says the thing could take six years to settle; then I had a fight with Mc-Ilhenny; and as if that were not enough, when I got back to my own office I had a fight with Bob. I feel bad about that—he was only trying to keep me from making a fool of myself, or worse—and I jumped down his throat for it."

"I know. Norma called before."

"Oh?"

"Mmmhmm. She said she had called Bob at the office to find out if we were going to their place tonight, and he told her what happened."

"And I suppose she told you?"

"Not really. At least I don't really understand what the fight was about. She just said that you chewed Bob out and that you were upset. What *did* you two argue about, anyway?"

"Wait a minute. Let me understand this. She called you just because I yelled at her husband? What did she think you were going to do, make me say I'm sorry?"

"Don't jump at me, Al. No, as a matter of fact she called to tell me that you were upset and that she understood about our not going to their house tonight. Then she suggested that you might want to reconsider—that we could all go out to a movie and have dinner out, if you wanted. Something to take your mind off your troubles."

"Nah, I don't really feel up to it. Frankly, all I want to do tonight is take off my shoes and relax in front of the television set."

"I sort of figured that. Why don't you go into the living room and turn on the news? Dinner will be ready in about fifteen minutes."

"Okay, Kath," Al Zimmerman said. "One thing, though."

"What's that?"

"If you get a chance between the salting and the stirring and the simmering, try saying a little prayer that the phone doesn't ring tonight. I've had enough for one day. I just couldn't take any more."

Twenty-five minutes later Zimmerman, seated at the dinner table, had just inserted the second forkful of mashed potato into his mouth when, naturally, the telephone rang. He looked knowingly at his wife as if to say that he had predicted it and, leaving his napkin on the table, he walked to the summoning instrument in the living room.

"Yeah? Zimmerman speaking," he said, picking up the receiver.

"Lieutenant? This is Sergeant Faraday. We've got a big one going on, and Captain McIlhenny said I should give you a call and see if you can come in."

"What's happening, Faraday? I just got home a little while ago."

"I don't know, sir. The captain didn't give me any of the details. He just asked me to call you and get you back here as soon as possible—if not sooner. It must be pretty important, I guess."

"Is he there, Sergeant? Captain McIlhenny? Can I talk to him?"

"He's here, sir, but he's pretty busy right now. As close as I can make out, there's been a big murder somewhere in our territory. The captain's already been on the phone to the Chief of Detectives and the Commissioner. Really, Lieutenant, all hell's breaking loose down here."

"Oh, all right," Zimmerman agreed reluctantly. "I'm on my way. I should be there in about forty minutes, more or less. Depends on the midtown tunnel."

"Good, sir. I'll tell the captain."

Hanging up the phone, Zimmerman turned and headed for the bedroom to retrieve his gun.

"Sorry about dinner, Kath," he called to his wife. "But you know how it is." Having strapped on his gun harness, he rebuttoned his shirt collar and tightened his necktie.

"I should after twenty-three years," Kathy replied. "What's going on?"

"Don't know. That was one of the night sergeants. He said the captain had already called the big brass, so I guess it must be important."

"Yeah. It's always important," she stated with an air of mild annoyance.

He shrugged his shoulders. "Look, I don't know what's happening yet, so I can't tell you when I'll be getting home. Don't wait up for me, though."

These were the same instructions he always gave her when he was called out at night—"Don't wait up for me"— yet she had always sat up waiting, only going to bed and pretending to be asleep when she heard his key turn in the door. In the twenty-three years they had been married, she had become something of an expert on the late-late movies, as well as on Sunrise Semester.

He slipped on his jacket and blew a kiss from the doorway as he left. She simply stared at the door after it closed behind him, then, sighing, went into the kitchen to get some plastic wrap to cover his dinner, wrapping the food on its plates against the wishful circumstance that he might return within an hour or two. A half hour later, when she had finished puttering around the kitchen and had picked at her own dinner until she gave up, having lost her appetite, she snapped on the television set in the living room and resigned herself to another night of waiting.

Everything appeared normal when Zimmerman entered the large entry hall of the Manhattan South Headquarters building. The first wave of the evening's drunk-and-disorderlies were being escorted through the paper trail that would lead them to the drunk tank for the night by a lesser number of patrolmen, and the sergeant at the desk was engaged, apparently as the intermediary, between a husband and wife who didn't seem to care for each other particularly. The desk sergeant glanced up helplessly at Zimmerman as he passed, blinking his eyes in acknowledgment of the lieutenant's half-wave.

But as soon as Zimmerman passed through the door marked HOMICIDE, the scene changed radically. Seemingly chaotic activity was all around him—at every desk, phones were ringing, typewriters were clattering, and policemen were conferring with each other, raising their voices to near shouts in order to be heard over the din of the room. Bypassing his own office, the lieutenant went directly to that of his captain. The door stood slightly ajar, so he entered without looking. Lou Esposito, the other lieutenant assigned to Manhattan Homicide South, was involved in a heated discussion with Captain McIlhenny. They both looked up as Zimmerman entered the room.

"Hi, Al," McIlhenny said. "Thanks for coming in."

Zimmerman nodded in acknowledgment and asked, "What's going on?"

"It's like a war, Al," Captain McIlhenny began. "People are getting shot up all over town. Apparently, it started over in Brooklyn. About two hours ago, one"—he paused to consult a sheet of paper in front of him—"Rico Bastitoni got himself shot as he was getting out of his car in front of a reputed horse room in Coney Island. Roughly twenty minutes later, Carlo Benante was shot down in a phone both outside a candy store near Prospect Park. Batistoni, by the way, was supposedly a member of the DeCarlo family, and Benante was a first cousin of the main branch of the Lorenzo tribe.

"Well, then it started to spread. Lessy Quinn staggered into a bar in Greenwich Village with a knife stuck in his back." Zimmerman's eyebrows raised at hearing a familiar name. "Madison's," the captain continued, naming the bar. "As you probably know, it's owned by Georgie Maducci, who is some kind of collateral cousin of Roberto Napoli, who also happens to be Quinn's father-in-law.

"Then, no more than an hour ago, Porkie Porcaro was dumped out of a car in front of Grossman's Restaurant on the Lower East Side. You know where is it—Avenue B or C, I forget, around Second Street. Porcaro worked as a muscleman for Carmine Antonuccio, and Grossman's is owned by the brother of Barry Grossman, Antonuccio's bookkeeper. Porcaro wasn't quite dead, although he is now. Before he died, he told the doorman that Napoli's boy Al DiGenoa had done it.

"About fifteen minutes ago, we got a call that DiGenoa had been found in an alley in the West Thirties with his belly cut open and his guts hanging out. They just took him over to Roosevelt Hospital—condition critical."

"It looks as if they're moving uptown and they're getting rougher," Zimmerman offered.

"That's how we see it," McIlhenny said, "so I called Peterson up at Manhattan North. He told me that it had already started up there. Some hood named Aaronson has been machine-gunned in front of the Park Regal Hotel. Two innocent bystanders were hit. Aaronson's dead, and so is an elderly man who was out walking his dog. The other bystander, a woman, was just taken to Mount Sinai in fair condition. Aaronson, by the way, has some tie-in to the DeCarlos in Brooklyn.

"They're killing each other so fast we can hardly keep up with the box score. Every time the phone rings, I think somebody else has gotten gunned down."

Zimmerman nodded that he understood. "What do you want me to do, sir?" he asked. Apparently, the captain was coordinating, so the lieutenant indicated that he awaited his orders.

"Well," the captain began, "we're rounding up everybody in town who has anything to do with the mobs—not because we've got anything to hold them on, but because they're going to get themselves killed if they stay on the street. Protective custody, sort of, until this thing calms down. As you know, we can hold them for forty-eight hours without charging them, and that's just what we intend to do.

"That's taking just about everybody, every available officer and detective, we can lay our hands on. You'd be surprised how many hoods there are in this town who are connected with the mobs. Well," he corrected himself, "maybe not surprised, but it is a colossal job to try to bring them all in at the same time. I've borrowed some troops from vice, narcotics, and tactical, and even with them, we've got our hands full.

"What I want you to do is take care of all the other business that comes in tonight. Faraday called Donofrio and he's on his way in, too, to give you a hand. With the Syndicate boys getting themselves killed tonight, somebody's got to mind the store in case some John Smith, respectable citizen type, decides that this is the night to do in his loving wife."

Zimmerman was visible shocked.

"Why me? Jesus, Mac, surely there are enough other people around to handle that. I mean, after all, if you've got a war going on, why are you putting me on rear-echelon duty?"

"Somebody's got to do it, Al. Why *not* you?"

"Because, because . . ." Zimmerman became tongue-tied.

"I suggest you get back to your office, Al. I've been putting the miscellaneous stuff on your desk and you've got some catching up to do. Donofrio should be in any minute now."

Captain McIlhenny turned away from the still standing Zimmerman and returned his attention to the papers he was going over with Lieutenant Esposito.

Zimmerman stood there, fuming at his curt dismissal, and stared at the other two policemen for a moment. Then he turned on his heel and stormed out of the captain's office and marched to his own, slamming the door behind him. As he plumped down into his chair, he was conscious that his ears were burning. For the first time in years, he felt that he was blushing with rage. He interpreted the captain's actions as a vote of "no confidence," and this had succeeded in infuriating him. The memory of an offer that had been made to him a few months ago to head the security division of a large corporation ran through his mind, along with the thought that perhaps he should not have been so hasty in turning it down.

"Hello, again," Sergeant Donofrio announced as he entered his superior's office.

"Oh, hi Bob," Zimmerman said as he snapped out of his reverie. He motioned for Donofrio to sit down. "Uh, Bob . . . I'm sorry if I lost my temper with you this afternoon. You know how it is."

"Sure. No sweat. Feeling better now?"

"As a matter of fact, I'm not. They've got the battle of the century going on in the streets, and we've gotten stuck with the shit detail."

Zimmerman then proceeded to explain to Donofrio what the captain had laid out for him a few minutes earlier.

"I'll tell you, Al," Donofrio concluded when Zimmerman had finished. "If you ask me, we're better off away from that."

"How so?"

"Nobody wins in those things. How long do you think it's going to take before the papers find a way of blaming the whole shoot-out on the police? You know, 'Police Powerless to Stop Gangland Gunplay,' that sort of thing. And when they quote some cop's weak answer to that charge, I'd rather it was McIlhenny than you or me. Let's face it, it's not going to do our noble captain's career any good."

"Maybe," Zimmerman said thoughtfully. "But I'm surprised at you. Frankly, I never realized that you were that much of a politician." There was nothing derogatory in the way Zimmerman said this; if anything, there was a note of grudging admiration for Donofrio's having seen an angle that he had overlooked.

"Why not?" Donofrio smiled. "Machiavelli was Italian, too, wasn't he?"

Zimmerman smiled back by way of reply. "Well, Bob," —he picked up four new files from his desk and passed two of them to the sergeant—"it looks as if people are still killing each other, even if they aren't members of the mobs." He opened one of the files himself. "Let's see what we've got tonight."

CHAPTER 15

IT WAS TWENTY-FIVE minutes after five that morning when Kathleen Zimmerman heard what sounded like her husband at the door to their apartment. In fact, the scuffling sound had awakened her. She had dozed off in the living-room armchair in the middle of a Randolph Scott Western that she had seen no fewer than four times before. Instantly alert, she gathered the milk glass and tin-foil leftover wrappings from the end table next to her chair in a single sweeping motion and deposited them in the kitchen on her way to the bedroom. Climbing quickly into bed, she pulled the covers up to her chin and closed her eyes.

But there was no sound of the key turning in the lock or of the door opening. Patiently, she waited, lying there with her eyes tightly shut. And waited. And waited.

After about five minutes, she made her decision and got out from under the bed linen, returning to the living room. Frankly puzzled about the very definite sounds she had heard at the door, she hesitated for a moment beside her chair, then went to the door to see if she could figure out what the noises had been.

Proceeding cautiously, she slid open the one-way-mirror peephole and squinted through the hole. All she could see was the wall opposite.

"Yes?" she asked. "Is anybody there?"

There was no reply.

Remembering her husband's warnings, she slipped the

chain onto the door and opened it as far as the restraint would allow—about four inches. The door felt heavier than usual, but she was still unable to see anything. She closed the door and removed the chain. Motivated by the sure knowledge that she would be unable to stop thinking about it until she had investigated thoroughly, she reopened the door wide.

At first, she was dumbstruck when the body that had been leaning on the door fell toward her. Instinctively, she reached out her arms to catch it before the man struck the floor. It was too heavy, though. She was able to keep the falling weight balanced upright for only a fraction of a second before it brushed by her and dropped to her foyer floor. She simply stared at the corpse lying at her feet, unable to grasp what had just happened. "I wish I could get Al to buy a suit like that," she thought disjointly as she surveyed the elegant pinstripe.

Then she was conscious of the clammy feeling at the front of her nightgown. Looking down at herself, she saw the dark smear of blood across her bodice reaching down almost to her waist. She held her hands out in front of her and perceived that they, too, were sticky with dark red. It was a full five minutes before her neighbors could stop her screaming.

CHAPTER 16

LIEUTENANT ALFRED ZIMMERMAN was more than a little surprised when he pulled his car into the garage at his apartment house at seven that morning and found his way blocked by a black-and-white patrol cruiser. The two uniformed policemen to whom the vehicle was assigned looked up with mild curiosity as he stopped his automobile about two feet from theirs and got out.

"What's going on?" Zimmerman asked brusquely.

The elder officer, a man in his mid-fifties with a waistline that almost matched his age in inches, ambled slowly toward Zimmerman.

"Sorry, buddy. This garage is closed. You'll have to find someplace else to park."

Zimmerman looked into the patrolman's face and mentally noted its intransigence.

"Why can't I park here? I live in this building."

"Look around you, buddy. I'll bet half the cars in here are police vehicles. We got to keep the area clear, that's all."

"Why? What's going on?"

The younger officer, sensing that his partner was not having too much success in getting rid of the intruder, began to walk to his side to reinforce his efforts.

"Police business," the younger man interjected. "Now move your car!" The two uniformed men stood side by side. The thought crossed Zimmerman's mind that to a civilian, they probably looked like the Los Angeles Rams front line. Reaching into his pocket, he produced his leather-encased badge.

"Zimmerman, Lieutenant, Police Department, City of New York," he identified, enunciating each word carefully. "Now will you please tell me what the hell is going on here?"

"Lieutenant?" the heavy-set policeman protested. "Why the hell didn't you say something about being on the force?"

"Did you really give me a chance? Now would you mind telling me what's happening?"

"Sorry, sir. There's been a murder. That's all I know. Benning here and me, we were just told to go down to the garage and keep the place clear for the meatwagon and the detectives. The wagon left. You just missed it. That's all I know, except that the detectives are still upstairs. You know how it is; when you're only a patrolman second class, nobody ever tells you anything." He shot a meaningful look at Zimmerman, his sharp stare saying that he was still annoyed at the lieutenant's not having identified himself immediately.

"Who was killed?"

"Don't know, sir. Why don't you ask the detectives?"

"Where are they?"

"Upstairs. Apartment Five-B, I think they said."

"Five-B?" Zimmerman asked, incredulous that the patrolman had identified his own apartment.

"That's right, Five-B."

"Oh, my God!" the lieutenant exclaimed and dashed to the elevator. He pushed the call button feverishly, trembling as he watched the floor indicator react slowly and swing counterclockwise from 5 down to G. He was perspiring freely when he heard the elevator stop in front of him. Pushing the door open, he entered and pushed the button labeled 5 with equal urgency. On the way up, the car paused at the first floor, but before the door could slide open, Zimmerman stopped it by pressing the Door Close button and the 5 button simultaneously. Reluctantly, the car resumed its ascent. He was tapping his foot impatiently on the floor when the elevator finally came to a halt at the fifth floor.

He leaped forward into the hallway before the door had slid completely open and found himself with no fewer than eight uniformed and plainclothes policemen milling around in the hall. Ignoring their "May I help you, sir's" and "Hey, wait a minute's," he charged through their midst to the portal of his home. The door was ajar, so he burst right through. His wife, and Sergeant Barry Conover, to whom she had been speaking, looked up in surprise.

"Al!" she declared, rushing toward him.

He allowed her to fall into his arms. "Kath, Kath," he repeated in relief. "When the patrolmen downstairs told me that there had been a murder in this apartment, I thought . . . I thought . . ." He hugged her tightly, reassuring himself that she was all right.

He did not know how long he held her, not thinking about anything other than the fact that she was safe. Finally, he loosened his grip and turned to the sergeant, who had been watching them patiently.

"Hello, Conover. What's going on?" He released his wife completely and took a step toward the sport-jacketed detective whom he had met casually once or twice when he had addressed training schools and once at a party given by a mutual friend. Sergeant Conover, Zimmerman recalled, was attached to Queens Homicide.

"Nothing to worry about, Lieutenant. As close as we can figure, it's part of this 'Shoot-out at OK Corral' that's been going on between the bad guys and the bad guys. Your wife, I'm afraid, found the body. I called you but you had already left Manhattan South."

Zimmerman glanced over at his wife, who was still shaken by her experience.

"The body was left right at your doorstep. Mrs. Zimmerman heard a noise and went out to investigate. That was about"—he paused to consult his note pad—"five-thirty this morning. We were here within twenty minutes. One of the neighbors, a Mr. Carroll, telephoned the local precinct and they turned it over to us."

"Who was the victim?" Zimmerman asked.

"Don't know, Lieutenant. We're running his fingerprints through Records now."

"Wasn't there any identification on the body?"

"Oh, there were things like clothing-store labels and laundry marks that we should be able to trace without too much trouble if we have to. But no wallet or credit cards or anything like that."

"Hmmph . . . Any guesses, Conover? As to either who he was or why he was left here?"

"Not really, Lieutenant. We should know who he is quickly enough. From the look of him, he was a hood of some kind. He had a Marine Corps tattoo on his right forearm, so if he doesn't have any kind of police record here, we should be able to track down his fingerprints through Washington. That'll tell us who he is. As to why he was deposited here, I was hoping you could tell us that."

"How should I know?" Zimmerman asked. "Do you at least have a picture of him?"

The sergeant reached into his inside jacket pocket and took out a Polaroid snapshot of the body which he offered to the lieutenant. Zimmerman took the picture from him and examined it carefully. Handing it back, he shook his head negatively. "Never seen him before."

"Well," the sergeant began speculating, "we really didn't think you would have. Although there's always that off-chance. . . ."

The lieutenant nodded.

"As close as we can figure it right now," Conover offered, "it's just another part of what's been going on since last night. You probably know more about it than I do. I understand the investigations are being coordinated out of Manhattan South. From the look of it, every Mafia family in New York is mad at every other family and they're killing each other off like the end of the world."

Rather than reveal that he had been relegated to a back seat in that investigation, Zimmerman merely shrugged his shoulders. "Yeah," he finally agreed, "They've been making out like it's World War Two on the streets. but in each case, as far as I can recall, there's some kind of tie-in between the body and the Organization. Each man killed has been found, pretty much, on his own doorstep. That is to say, his body was sent back to his family. Why should they break that pattern to leave this guy's body with me?"

"Who knows, Lieutenant? We may not see it, but I'm sure there was some kind of reason. You know *them*. They never do anything without a reason."

Zimmerman looked into the eyes of the investigating officer. The sergeant's expression clearly stated that he believed Zimmerman knew something that he wasn't telling.

"Hey, come on, Barry," Zimmerman protested. "I know that look. I should—I've used it often enough myself. Why don't you tell me just what it is that you think I know, or what it is that you don't believe, and I'll see if I can help you."

"Well, sir, it's just that I know there has to be a good explanation for the body left here at your apartment. Let's face it—it couldn't have been an accident. No chance. The murderer had to bring the body into the building. He was killed someplace else, by the way. Nobody in the apartment house heard any shots and the examining medical man said that the man had been dead about an hour when he was left here—he could tell from the degree of clotting, or lack of it, of the blood. That would make the time of death four-thirty this morning. And after he brought the body into the building, he had to come up to this floor, choose a place to dump his load, and then leave without being detected. Now that's quite a risk for him to take if all he was trying to do was get rid of a body. Look, suppose you were in his position and you had a corpse you were trying to lose somewhere. You'd pick some nice out-of-the-way spot and dump it there, right? Maybe some alleyway or basement, or garage, or even the river. You wouldn't go to all the trouble of carting it to a cop's door, would you? Not unless you had some damn good reason to do so, huh?"

"I suppose you're right," Zimmerman said. He had, of course, recognized all this before the sergeant had launched into his explanation, and had only listened halfheartedly, preferring to concentrate on trying to figure out just what that elusive reason could have been. "Do me favor, Conover. When you figure out what that reason was, give me a call and let me know. Now, if you're all finished here, I haven't been to sleep in I don't know how long, and to tell you the truth, I'm dead on my feet. So if you don't mind, I'm going to sack out for a while. Okay?"

"Sure, Lieutenant," the sergeant answered in mild surprise. "We're just about done here anyway."

Zimmerman's wife followed him into the bedroom. She watched silently as he stripped off his tie and shirt. He seated himself on the edge of the bed to remove his shoes prior to taking off his trousers. As he dropped the second shoe to the floor, he looked up at her. "Yeah, Kath? Is something on your mind?"

"Why, Al? Why would they leave some strange body here? The sergeant is right—there has to be an explanation."

Al Zimmerman stood as he unbuckled his belt and unzipped his fly. He looked at her thoughtfully as he removed his trousers. Standing now in his underwear, he said, "I really don't know, Kath. But you're right—there must be an explanation. Whatever it is," he yawned, "I'll find it." He swung his legs up onto the bed. "Don't worry about it, though. It's probably something so simple that we can't see it." He yawned again and allowed his torso to slope back until his head was touching the pillow. "Nothing to worry about, though," he mumbled as he drifted off to sleep. "Nothing to worry . . ."

CHAPTER 17

"How's it going? I'll tell you how it's going," Zimmerman said in response to Bob Donofrio's casual inquiry. "Do you remember when we had that guy from NYU giving that seminar a few months ago and he told us that sometimes it's more important to figure out what questions to ask than to worry about the answers? Do you remember? He said that if you ask the right questions, they'll help you get to the real roots of the problem."

"Yeah, I remember."

"Well, he didn't know what the hell he was talking about. I suspected as much at the time, but what he said did seem to make a little sense, so I kept my mouth shut. Now I can tell you in no uncertain terms: that jerk was all wet."

"What's the matter, Al?" Donofrio asked placatingly, raising his eyebrows at his colleague's rancor.

"All I've got is questions!" Zimmerman bristled. "No answers, just questions. And until I start getting some answers, I'm going nuts."

"Like what?"

"Like, why was my brother murdered? Like, what triggered this gang warfare we've been going through? Like, why, all of a sudden, does my brother's insurance company decide that they don't have to pay off on his life insurance? Like, where in the name of God am I supposed to find the money to pay my sister-in-law's bills and how is she supposed to feed two kids without any money coming in? Like, why, in the midst of all this mess, does a body get deposited at my door at five A.M. last night? Like, what the hell is going on, anyway?"

"Hey, take it easy. Take it easy, Al. I know you're upset, but flying off the handle won't help. Maybe if we take these things one at a time, we can make some sense of them."

"Sure, sure," Zimmerman agreed.

"Okay. Now, first, why was your brother murdered? I thought everybody agreed that it was over some book-maker's debt. In fact, why don't you throw in another question, and ask why the "collector" called to get payment after he had been murdered? We've both been policemen for a long time and neither of us has ever heard of anything like that before—the Organization killing somebody and then trying to collect from his widow. So that would cast some doubt over the assumption that he was killed over a gambling debt, wouldn't it?

"Now I can't see how your first question and your second question—why the gang war?—are related. Maybe they are, but I can't see it. I just can't see that your brother was a big-enough wheel to warrant this kind of response, if it was a gangland killing. So let's eliminate the gangster business, at least in terms of this rash of killings, altogether."

"But . . ." Zimmerman tried to interject.

"Wait a minute and let me finish. Next question, why won't the insurance company pay off? That's simple. They probably see the same thing that that lawyer explained. That is, there might be a way they can put off paying for a few years and thus continue to use that money. It sounds inhuman, I grant, but that's the way they operate. Who was it—Ian McHarg, I think—who said that a businessman is someone who can look at a slum and only see a business investment? That's the way it is, Al."

"You and your night courses!"

Donofrio smiled at the gibe. "Okay, where you're going to get the money to support your brother's family until the insurance company pays off, I don't know. But let me advise you of this—do you know that she can collect a couple of hundred dollars a month from Social Security for the kids? I think they'll pay until the kids turn eighteen. And if they're in college, I think they pay until age twenty-two. That lawyer should be able to advise you on that. Now, as a friend, I'll add this—I know it's still going to be rough, even with Social Security payments, so if you need a couple of thousand, I'll take it out of my savings and loan it to you."

"That's very nice of you, Bob, but I really couldn't. It isn't your problem, after all."

"Let me be the judge of what's my problem. Now then, to get back to the questions without answers, the one question that doesn't seem to fit is why they decided to drop that body at your apartment. Even if it was a part of the gang war, it doesn't seem to make any sense. If it wasn't a part of that, if, in fact, it was an independent action, it makes even less sense. So that's really the only question that we don't have any answer for—why was that body dumped with you?"

Donofrio, having finished his discourse, looked at his friend meaningfully.

"Are you done?" Zimmerman inquired.

Donofrio nodded that he was.

"Good. Now let me poke some holes in your arguments. First, whether we agree with it or not, there is a lot of substantiation for assuming that my brother's murder was tied to some gambling debt, so let's operate on that assumption. Snyder buys it, and he's in charge of the case. Now let's jump to the end and also assume that the body was left at my apartment last night for a reason. I have no idea what that reason might be, but I don't think anybody believes that it was an accident—that the Mafia, or whatever you want to call them, dumped a stiff on my doorstep for no good reason. There were too many easier places for them to get rid of it. Also, I don't know if you noticed it, but the method was very similar to the way my brother's body was found. Oh, there are differences, all right, but both bodies were put right at the front door."

"But your brother was murdered there. From what I heard, the body that was dropped off last night was killed earlier and simply deposited in front of your door."

"I said there are differences, but I think they're out-weighed by the similarities. In fact, although I acknowledge that my brother was pretty small stuff and certainly didn't rate a gang war on his behalf, all the bodies—at least all that I heard about, not being assigned to the case—were dropped rather conspicuously. The only relationship I have to all this, the only reason for them to dump a body at my door would be if it had something to do with my brother. Look, I've had the occasional run-in with organized crime in my career, but not for a long time and, let's face it, I just plain haven't been all that successful in catching hired guns. To the best of my knowledge, the Mafia has no reason to bear me a grudge, or at least no more so than any other cop. Yet they selected me for this singular honor. Why, if it didn't have something to do with my brother?"

Before Donofrio could speculate on an answer, the door opened and Captain McIlhenny ducked his head in the room. "How are you two doing on the Dunway murder?" the captain asked.

"The woman who was stabbed to death last night?" Zimmerman answered. "Her husband did it. We've got him in custody. The airport police picked him up at JFK trying to catch a plane to Europe."

The captain's thick features spread in mild surprise. He ran his right fingers through the shock of unruly sandy hair, now mixed with gray, that topped his freckled face. "You've

92

already made an arrest?"

"Well, we're holding him on suspicion of murder."

"What kind of evidence have you got?"

Zimmerman opened a file on his desk and glanced through it quickly.

"I can't really tell you, sir. The paperwork hasn't really caught up yet. He was just brought in a couple of hours ago."

"Have you interrogated him yet?"

"Not personally. I only got here about twenty minutes ago myself. But the murder weapon, a carving knife, was found in the apartment. We're cross-matching the fingerprints on it with his right now."

"Well, I hope you've got more than that to go on," McIlhenny said emphatically. "Any defense lawyer worth his salt could give you a dozen reasons why a man's fingerprints might be on his own carving knife, you know."

"Don't worry, Captain. We're piecing it all together. From the look of this one, we'll be able to hand it to the District Attorney on a silver platter."

Captain McIlhenny had opened his mouth to respond, but before he could do so, the phone rang.

"Excuse me, Captain," Zimmerman said as he lifted the receiver.

"Homicide, Zimmerman speaking, Oh, yeah, Conover. What've you got? Good. You better spell that." He fumbled for a pencil and paper. "Okay, D-I-B-E-N-N-I-D-E-T-T-O, Daniel. a/k/a Fancy Dan Benedict. That's his name, but who was he? You're still checking that? Okay, let me know when you've got something. Huh? No, no, I never heard of him, much less met him. Yeah, that's what he sounds like to me, too. Sure, sure. If I think of any connection I'll give you a ring. Thanks for calling, Barry. Right. Bye."

Zimmerman hung up the phone and looked up at his superior officer. "They identified the guy who was dumped on my doorstep last night, Captain. Some small-time hood named Daniel DiBennidetto. Lived in Brooklyn. They're still waiting for the coroner's report and all that stuff. You might want to add that to your file of last night's casualties."

"Al," McIlhenny began cautiously, "why don't you do us both a favor and take a few days of sick leave?"

"What?"

"Al, I can see it happening. Now you're getting wrapped up in this DiBennidetto murder. Queens Homicide knows what it's doing. They don't need your help."

"Mac," Zimmerman said, struggling to control his temper. "You seem to forget that DiBennidetto's body was found outside my aparment. Queens Homicide is only following good, established procedure and asking me if I know anything that can aid them in their investigation. If I'm curious about it, I think that's a forgivable reaction. After all, I don't receive gift-wrapped bodies every day."

"If you've got so much curiosity," McIlhenny bridled, "why don't you use a little of it on the Dunway case? From what I can see, you've hardly done your homework there. How's it going to look if we have to let the husband go on a habeas corpus writ because you couldn't spare the time to build a prima facie case?"

"We've already got a prima facie case. We've got a motive—Dunway's wife had at least two boyfriends that the neighbors volunteered information about—we've got the murder weapon, and we picked him up trying to flee the country."

"Sure, and Dunway's got a lawyer, I'll bet, who can get him sprung within forty-eight hours on that kind of case. We need evidence, Al, and you know it. Did anybody hear them fighting? Did he ever threaten her? Have you located these so-called boyfriends. For all you know, they were her brothers come to pay a visit to their loving sister. You're still a long way from home with Dunway, and if you'd stop to think about it, you'd agree with me. Believe me, I'm not going to blow that case and watch a murderer walk away a free man because the lieutenant I put in charge of the investigation was too busy with cases that were none of his business to do a proper job of putting together evidence."

"Okay, Mac." Zimmerman raised his voice as the vestiges of control disappeared from his temper. "Let's hear it all. You've been acting like you wouldn't trust me with issuing a traffic citation ever since my brother was killed. You chewed me out the other day about getting too close to that investigation, when in fact I haven't been anywhere near it; then last night you called me in just to hand me all the crap jobs while everybody else was working on an undeclared war. If you don't trust me, if you don't think I can handle my job, why don't you just say so and get it out in the open. Manhattan North has needed another lieutenant ever since Halliday retired last month. If you don't trust me here, maybe it's time for me to put in for a transfer."

"Calm down, Al," McIlhenny said placatingly, seating himself on the edge of Zimmerman's desk. "Nobody said they don't trust you. I am worried about you, though. You're one of the best cops I've ever worked with and I'm proud to have you in my command. But I've seen it happen before, and I don't want it to happen to you. Do you remember Harry Benson over in the Bronx? He was a good cop, too. Then his son got clobbered by a hit-and-run driver. Crippled for life. Benson couldn't accept the fact that it might have been an accident. Long after Traffic had written the case off, he kept on it. It was as if it possessed him and he couldn't let up. Of course, all his other work went down the tubes just as yours is starting to do. He convinced himself that whoever hit his son had done so deliberately, Al. And he never stopped looking for the guy. He never found him, of course. But he kept right on looking. At one point, he started going around to every punk he had ever rousted and roughed them up because he was convinced that one of them would be able to tell him who had tried to get even with him through his son. Well, it had to happen. He was bouncing some nickle-dime hood off a wall and he fractured the guy's skull. When he realized what he had done, he cracked entirely. He's still in Bronx County, Al. The last I heard, he'll probably spend the rest of his life in the psychiatric ward there.

"I was talking to Jeff Cowan, who was his captain, last year and he told me about a visit to Benson. The guy goes around the hospital asking all the orderlies if they've seen a green Buick with a broken headlight. That's all he does. Outside of that, he can't even go to the bathroom by himself.

"I need you too much here, Al. Until you can clear your mind of your brother's murder, I'm not going to trust you with anything that even remotely resembles organized crime. And I'm certainly not going to condone your investigating your brother's case yourself. That's why I say, why don't you take some sick leave and try to snap out of it? I know you just got back from vacation. Go back to the mountains. The clean air will help you clear your head of all this. Now, what do you say?"

"Let me give it some thought, Mac," Zimmerman said softly.

"Okay, Al. Promise me you'll think about it," McIlhenny asked as he rose to leave.

"Sure, Mac. And, Mac?"

"Yeah?"

"Thanks."

Neither Zimmerman nor Donofrio spoke for a moment after the captain's visit. The lieutenant remained behind his desk, staring at his hands folded in front of him. His subordinate sat looking at him expectantly.

Finally, Zimmerman looked up, his eyes meeting Donofrio's gaze. "Where were we?" he asked.

"I beg your pardon?" Donofrio asked.

"We were trying to put together some of the pieces of whatever it is that's going on. Now as I see it, the only reason they would have left DiBennidetto's body with me is that his death and my brother's death are somehow related. Establishing just what that relationship—"

"Al! Weren't you listening?" his friend demanded. "Mc-Ilhenny just finished telling you to stay away from that case."

"Establishing just what that relationship was," Zimmerman continued insistently, "is the real problem."

Donofrio shrugged his shoulders in semiresignation and added a weak protest: "Al, Mac might just have a point, you know. After all, they don't let a surgeon operate on a member of his family. I can't see how this is different. Hell, they told us in our first week at the Police Academy not to get emotionally involved in our cases."

"Bob," Zimmerman explained, "this is something that I have to do. Can't you guys understand that?"

Before Donofrio could respond, the telephone rang.

"Homicide, Zimmerman," the lieutenant said.

"Yeah, Barry. What've you got now? What? Tortured? You're kidding!" He paused in silence as his caller supplied the details. "I'll be damned. What do you guys make of it? No, I have no idea why. Yeah. UnHunh. Okay. Talk to you later. Thanks for calling."

The lieutenant carefully replaced the telephone receiver on its cradle and looked up at Donofrio.

"This case, as somebody once said, is getting curiouser and curiouser. That was Barry Conover over in Queens again. The coroner's report just came in on DiBennidetto. Would you believe that he had apparently been tortured before they killed him? His hands. Every finger had been broken, very carefully and methodically. Each finger was broken in the same place, as if somebody had placed it in a vise and kicked his feet out from under him. Whew!"

Zimmerman looked at Donofrio questioningly, as if to ask if the sergeant saw any explanation for this new development. Donofrio simply looked back at his lieutenant noncommittally.

"Well," Zimmerman speculated as he thought out loud, "this certainly ties it to the Mafia. Nobody else that I've ever heard of in this country still uses tortures like that. Now, my brother's wrist was sprained. I wonder if there's anything that ties those two things together?" Zimmerman paused, then said, "No, I don't think so. The doctor said that that was as if it had been twisted or wrenched or jammed. No hint of torture.

"No, from what I can remember about the Organization, when they do something like this, it's usually symbolic. I remember one case, oh, maybe ten or twelve years ago, in which we found some hood who had been sexually mutilated—castrated, in fact—and left to die. He never told us anything before he did die the next day, but we were able to establish through the grapevine that he had been playing around with the daughter of one of the big cheeses in the organization. And then there was Rocco D'Alesio a couple of years ago, if you recall. He testified against one of the Buono boys. They found him with his tongue cut out."

Donofrio nodded to indicate that he remembered the case.

"Now, perhaps if we could figure out what the broken fingers symbolized, we'd start getting somewhere," Zimmerman said.

"Maybe it means DiBennidetto was greedy," Donofrio suggested. "You know, like he had his hand in the till?"

"Could be," Zimmerman agreed. "Or perhaps he beat up somebody he shouldn't have—you know, beat up . . . hands?"

"Maybe."

"There are probably a lot of explanations, if we sat down and thought about them. If only there were some way I could find out for sure."

"Oh, yeah," Donofrio said sarcastically, "I'm sure if you asked them, they'd tell you. Let's face it, Al, the only way you're ever going to learn anything with any degree of certainty will be if somebody who knows decides to tell you. And I don't think there's too much of a chance of that happening."

Zimmerman looked at Donofrio thoughtfully. "You might have a point there, Bob. Maybe I should go and ask them."

"Hey, I was kidding! You can't penetrate the Organization. And they're sure as hell not going to come to you."

"I don't know about that, Bob. Oh, I don't expect them to come to me, but there's still that guy who wants the two thousand bucks. I'll bet I could get him to lead me to whomever he works for. That's a start, anyway."

"Are you back on that kick? Besides, I have my doubts as to whether you ll be hearing from him again."

"Why's that?"

"Well, he was supposed to call back in two weeks, remember? It's been almost three weeks now, and you haven't heard. I have a feeling that whoever it was was trying a shot in the dark to see if he could make some fast money, and then thought better of it. Maybe he heard that the insurance company wasn't going to pay off."

"How could he have found that out?"

"How should I know? One thing's for sure, though—when the Organization wants information, they usually get it."

"Hmmph," the lieutenant declared, having come to a dead end in his logical inquiry. "Well, no matter how I look at it, I still need more information. And that information is all contained in the deep, dark reaches of the Organization."

Zimmerman looked at his friend appraisingly. Then he lowered his eyes to the desk and began hesitantly: "Uh,

Bob . . . I wonder . . . I mean, the only Organization hoods I have had any contact with are all pretty low level. That is, you know, hired thugs, the occasional numbers runner, once in a while some petty bookie or pimp. I have no idea who any of the big wheels are, or at least not any more than I read in the newspapers. You know, 'reputed Mafia chieftain Joe Doakes' and that sort of thing. I don't suppose that you . . . ?"

"That I what, Al?" Donofrio bristled, his dark skin turning a deep gray. "Say what you're thinking."

"Well, uh, you wouldn't know who any of the big shots are, would you?"

"You're right," he replied indignantly. "I wouldn't know who any of the Mafia big guns are. Why should I? Because I'm Italian? I thought I knew you better than that. We've been friends for quite a while. You should have let me know that you thought of me as just another guinea gangster!" He spat the words out with a fury that Zimmerman had never before seen in him.

"Hey, Bob, don't get me wrong. I never said that I grouped you with them. And I certainly don't think that way."

"Oh? It certainly sounded like it a second ago."

"Bob, Bob, as you just said, we're friends. Do us both a favor and don't take offense when none was intended."

"I'll have to think about it," said Donofrio as he rose and left the room quickly. "You'll have to pardon me, but I've got some follow-up work to do on the Dunway case. It might not be a bad idea if you got busy on some of your real workload yourself."

Zimmerman, alone in his office now, uttered an audible sigh and said to no one, "I can't win for losing, can I?"

CHAPTER 18

SERGEANT ROBERT DONOFRIO did not say anything to his superior officer when he marched into Zimmerman's office two mornings later. He simply tossed a carefully folded sheet of paper on the lieutenant's desk, turned, and left. Zimmerman watched Donofrio leave before he picked up the paper and opened it. On it was written: "Thomas Holland, 2119 Hicks Street, Brooklyn." He turned the sheet over to see if anything was written on the reverse side, but nothing was. Walking to the door, he stood there trying to catch Donofrio's eye without making a point of it. Finally, he cleared his throat and the sergeant looked up. Zimmerman beckoned him to return to his office.

They were both seated before the lieutenant spoke: "Bob, I'm sorry about the other day. I certainly didn't mean any offense."

"Well, Lieutenant, maybe I'm getting sensitive in my old age," Donofrio replied with a weak smile.

Zimmerman winced, both at his friend's having addressed him by his rank, a formality the two friends had dispensed with years earlier, and at the reference to age. He was eleven years older than Donofrio, and on days like this, he felt every day of it.

"Who's Holland?" he asked, shifting the subject.

"I did some checking. As far as I can tell, he's pretty high up in the Brooklyn Organization. He many even be the top dog himself. I don't know for sure, and neither do my informants. They just know that he's up there in the big leagues."

"Is there any file on him down in Records, or haven't you had a chance to check yet?"

"Oh, I checked, all right. As soon as I got here this morning. That's why I'm a little late. To answer your question, though, there's nothing on any Thomas Holland. But I had a thought and looked up 'Olanda,' you know, Olanda, Holland, and I struck paydirt."

He removed some jumbled scraps of notepaper from his inside jacket pocket.

"Here we go. Olanda, Thomas. Born Brooklyn, 1912; attended Catholic schools in Brooklyn until he went off to Columbia in 1928." He paused and looked up to editorialize: "Must be pretty bright, going to college at sixteen." He returned to the notes. "Graduated with honors in 1932; took an MBA at Harvard in '33.

"Now we start coming to the interesting stuff. In late 1933, after Mr. Olanda had been awarded his distinguished degree, he went to work for Dobler Trucking and Warehouse Corporation, headquartered in Brooklyn. His first job was as an accountant. That was where he had his first run-in with the police. In February of '35, Internal Revenue was trying to nail one Felice Caputo, who happened to be the chairman of the board of Dobler. They knew that Dobler used to run tank trucks—they look like regular vans, but they have false bottoms and fronts that held tanks—a standard semivan could hold almost a thousand gallons of booze in addition to its legitimate cargo—but they couldn't make it stick. Caputo's organization must have had a good intelligence system, because every time the Treasury agents hit one of his vans, it was clean. Yet they were convinced Caputo had been a rumrunner, so they took the next-best route and tried to get him on income-tax evasion. They had him, too, until Olando entered the picture. The defense pulled him as a surprise witness at the trial, and he stood up and testified that it was he who had fouled up the books. He even showed them where he made his mistakes. In fact, he showed them some bookkeeping tricks he had used that weren't quite legal but could appear to have been honest errors. Subtracting figures instead of adding them, that sort of thing. Well, to make a long story short, that got Caputo off the hook. Oh, they slapped him with restitution plus interest on the unpaid taxes, but there was more than enough reasonable doubt for him to be free from any punitive action. Olanda knew that he was marked by the Treasury people then, so he simply disappeared. Ceased to exist. There's no sign of him anywhere after that.

"Okay, where does that leave us? In 1935 with a dead-end, right?" Donofrio looked very pleased with himself. "Wrong!" he declared. "When I ran out of data on our friend Olanda, I called a guy I know over at One twenty Church Street—the Internal Revenue Service. Maybe you remember him—Andy Pulaski, we worked with him on that Henderson case a few years ago—and I asked him to open his file on Thomas Holland to me. I went over there after work yesterday—it's only a couple of blocks from here, if you recall, and I must say, I was intrigued by what I learned. It seems that Thomas Holland came into existence in 1935 in Cincinnati. No tax records before that point, and his Social Security card wasn't issued until then. Yet his first job was President of the Ohio Chemical Corporation. That's really starting at the bottom, wouldn't you say? President of the company! He stayed there until 1942, when he left to take over the presidency of Independent Products in Detroit. Independent Products had a diverse product line, as you might imagine from the name, and during the war they made butt-plates for some of our rifles, so Holland was draft-exempt. Even if he had been draftable, when you think about it, they couldn't have gotten him because he didn't exist. Selective Service would have sent its Greetings to Thomas Olanda.

"All right, when the war ended, Holland set up an operation in London called American Investment, Ltd. He decided to promote himself at that point and instead of president, he became chairman of the board. He sort of disappeared from the tax records, because he was overseas. But he reappeared in 1951 as the president of San Francisco Food Corporation, an outfit that operates a fleet of tuna boats with canneries in the States, Mexico, Chile, and Guatemala.

"I'll skip a couple of interim presidencies in L.A. and Chicago, and bring you up to date. He returned to New York, Brooklyn—actually, in 1966 and assumed his present position as president of the Algonquin Corporation."

Zimmerman, who had been growing a little bored with Donofrio's monologue, perked up at this information. It was the first company that the sergeant had mentioned that had a familiar name. "Algonquin Corporation," the lieutenant asked, "that's one of those giant financial holding companies, isn't it?"

"Right!" the sergeant responded. "And you'll never guess the names of some of the companies they 'hold.' For one, they have a controlling interest in Dobler Trucking, which changed its name in 1936 to Ramparts Transport, and believe it or not, in one way or another, they control every company for which the eminent Mr. Holland worked. Oh, it's complicated enough. Treasury has been trying to build a case against them for years, but so far, they're clean. It's the sort of thing where San Francisco Foods owns twenty percent of Independent Products, and Algonquin owns another twenty percent outright, and Ohio Chemical owns yet another fifteen percent, which results in Algonquin actually controlling over fifty percent. As often as not, according to Pulaski, the remaining thirty or forty percent is publicly

104

traded, in order to keep money flowing into the captive companies. It also sets a value for the stock that the holding company retains, should it ever decide to sell any of it."

"All right," Zimmerman said. "I can see some ties between Holland and Caputo, and the relationship, possibly, between Holland and Olanda. But is there anything that ties all this to the Organization now?"

"Not directly. They're much too careful for that. The last thing they want is to have a straightlaced outfit like Algonquin linked to the seamy side of life—gambling, prostitution, and narcotics. And they're loyal to a fault. For example, one of San Francisco Foods' tuna boats was impounded last year and found to hold twenty-four kilos of cocaine in addition to fish. The captain swore up and down that the company didn't know anything about it. He drew five to ten, the maximum sentence on a first offense, yet he never said a word about having been acting on orders from upstairs.

"But one thing is certain, and the Treasury boys are working on this now: Algonquin would be a beautiful place for the rackets to get rid of black money—you know, excess profits that they can't account for. It's a natural setup for that sort of thing."

"When does Treasury think they'll be able to prove it?"

"It could take years, Al. Years. These corporate structures alone are so complicated that it has taken them almost three years to figure out what I just told you. They estimate it might be at least two more years before they have enough evidence to go before a grand jury. You have to realize that there are eighteen companies involved here, with assets totaling well over a billion dollars. What's more, the companies, in their dealings with each other, are clean to the point of absurdity. In fact, they take pains *not* to deal with each other whenever possible, but to go through third parties, like independent distributors and brokers.

After all, they don't want to get the Securities Exchange Commission down on them."

"Bob," Zimmerman began, obviously impressed with the amount of research his associate had accomplished in a very short time, "there's one thing I'm curious about. How did you stumble on Holland, or Olanda's name in the first place? I mean, this is a very carefully concealed operation, and you seem to have cracked it just by knowing which man held the key."

Donofrio looked at his superior with disappointment. "I'll tell you the truth, Al, I just lucked out. I called a cousin of mine who grew up on the same block with a minor branch of the Anastasias, figuring he might have some gossip. He said that Holland was the highest-ranking Organization man he had heard of but that he really didn't know much about him. On a long shot, I checked out Olanda, and you know what I found. Satisfied?"

Al Zimmerman smiled. "I was just curious, Bob."

"Sure." Donofrio returned the smile, as if determined not to allow Zimmerman's frayed nerves to ruin a good friendship. "By the way, Al. Just to satisfy your curiosity a little more, take a guess at what other company is controlled by Algonquin."

"I have no idea."

"Champlain Insurance Company!"

CHAPTER 19

AFTER IMPRISONING New York for almost a month in saunalike drought, the heat had finally subsided. It had rained torrentially all night, and when Al Zimmerman emerged from his apartment house the next morning, he felt a distinct chill in the air. Instead of the morning haze to which he had become accustomed, he was able to see clearly the high clouds racing across the city sky—the first hint that autumn was not very far away. As he drove toward Brooklyn, he spotted a billboard clock thermometer which informed him that the time was eight twenty-one and the temperature fifty-eight degrees, courtesy of the friendly folks at the Metropolitan Commercial National Bank. Reacting to this data, he reached with his right hand and, for the first time since June, flicked on his car heater. Before he had traveled another mile, he was forced to roll down his window partway to combat the steady draft of hot air rising from under the dashboard. For the remainder of the trip, he fiddled unsuccessfully with the heater controls and the window to reach a comfortable temperature.

Turning from the main thoroughfare onto Hicks Street, Zimmerman began his search for address numbers in order to find 2119. He found 2101, a huge, new concrete-and-glass structure that resembled a pile of uneven blocks stacked by a slightly astigmatic four-year-old, then 2121, an earlier, slightly more elegant tower with a faded yellow-tan facade of brick. The elegance was lost as soon as the observer got beyond the quoins to the sides of the building, which were made of large, cheap-looking blocks of indeterminate material.

In the gully between the two apartment houses, standing like a midget between a pair of professional basketball players, was 2119 Hicks Street, a pseudo-brownstone single-family residence, a scant three stories high.

Lieutenant Alfred Zimmerman pulled his car to the curb opposite the small building, parking barely inches from a fire hydrant. As he got out, he automatically flipped the sun visor down, revealing his police identification to any passing patrolman who might be tempted to ticket the vehicle.

As he approached the building, he saw that it was not built of the traditional sandstone or limestone at all, but of brick. It had achieved its dull brown color through a century of soot and smog. The entranceway, by contrast was newly painted, with gleaming brass ornamentation. A small polished plaque revealed in graceful script that this, indeed, was the Holland residence.

Zimmerman pulled the bell plunger and waited patiently for a reply. He was about to pull the knob again when the door opened and revealed an impeccably groomed man of late middle age wearing a midnight-blue suit and dark tie. Without having to be told, Zimmerman knew that this was the butler.

"Yes?"

"I'd like to see Mr. Holland, please," the policeman said.

The servant scanned the caller rapidly from haircut to shoes. Zimmerman found himself briefly wondering whether his shoes were properly shined. He knew that his trousers could use a pressing.

"Mr. Holland is not at home, sir. Do you have an appointment?"

"No, but I think he'll see me. When do you expect him back?"

The butler again glanced at Zimmerman's off-the-rack $49.95 suit with a certain disdain and said, "I'm not at all sure. If you would like to leave your card, I'm sure Mr. Holland will be in touch if he requires your services."

"He thinks I'm a door-to-door salesman," the policeman thought.

"Is he at his office? If you'll tell me where that is, I can contact him there. Although I'm sure he'd rather see me in the privacy of his own home."

"Perhaps if you told me the nature of your business, sir, I could be of some help," the butler offered. "Mr. Holland has placed me in charge of all the household accounts, you see."

"It's a personal matter," Zimmerman allowed, growing slightly impatient. Then, sarcastically imitating the butler's extra careful, slightly English pronunciation, he said, "You see, I'm with the police." Having announced this fact, Zimmerman took out his leather-encased badge and held it approximately six inches from the servant's face.

The man paused, as if he had to think for a moment. Then he opened the door the rest of the way and said, "If you'll just come this way, sir, I believe I may be able to locate Mr. Holland." Walking behind the butler, Zimmerman marveled that such things as butlers still existed. In many of the murder mysteries he had read as a boy, butlers had figured prominently. Yet, in his twenty-three years of police work, this was the first one he had met.

"If you'll wait in here, sir," the butler indicated, waving toward a sitting room, "I'll see if I can find Mr. Holland." The butler was gone before Zimmerman could either agree or disagree.

Alone now in the elegant room, Zimmerman examined its furnishings like an auctioneer appraising antiques. His wife had magazines filled with pictures of rooms like this, yet he was overwhelmed by the fact that such places were also to

109

be found in the real world. A place for everything and everything in its place, he thought, as he studied his surroundings. His eyes fell on a table of some French origin that escaped him. One of the Louis, he recalled, but that was as close as he could come to identifying it. What he did remember was that a similar piece had been pictured in the Sunday *Times,* with a caption that it had sold at auction for over thirty thousand dollars. His eyes fell on the oriental carpet beneath his feet. Its rich, inch-thick pile felt strangely luxurious under his feet as he walked on it. Kathy, he thought, could spend her life in such a room without wanting to leave.

The man who quietly entered the room matched the furnishings as much as any of the lamps or chairs.

"How may I help you?" Thomas Holland asked. "I understand you're with the police."

His sweater, Zimmerman thought, cost more than my suit. There was no resentment in this notion, however. Zimmerman knew that he could never attain such sartorial heights.

"My name is Zimmerman, Mr. Holland. I'm a lieutenant in Homicide." The policeman kept his eyes on Holland's face to see if any flicker of recognition was betrayed at his name. There was none—only an expression of mild surprise at his specialty.

"Homicide? Lieutenant, has someone been killed?"

"It's a long story, Mr. Holland. Yes, I'm investigating a murder. I think you may be able to help us fit some of the pieces together."

"I can't think how, Lieutenant, but I'm only too happy to cooperate in any way I can." Then, as if remembering his manners, he said, "Please sit down." Choosing a straight-backed wing chair for himself, he slipped his frame into it as facilely as a rifle bolt closing in the breech. Zimmerman sat down gingerly on the edge of an upholstered side chair, convinced that his mass would send its spindly legs splintering across the floor. The chair held, however, without as much as a squeak of protest, so the lieutenant began: "Mr. Holland, I'm investigating the murder of one Arnold Zimmerman of Forty-two-forty-four East Sixteenth Street, Brooklyn, on the eighteenth of August this year."

Holland's brow furrowed in thought. "Zimmerman, Zimmerman . . . Was he an employee of Algonquin Corporation? Frankly, I don't recognize the name, other than to observe that it's the same as your own. Why don't you get hold of Perry Bradley? He's the personnel director at our corporate headquarters. I'm sure he'll be happy to cooperate with the police. You may tell him I gave you his name."

"No, Mr. Holland. Arnold Zimmerman was not one of your employees. He was my brother. Not that one would exclude the other, but as it happens, he didn't work for any of your companies."

Holland appeared to be at a loss. "Then why are you asking me . . . ?" His posture changed as he leaned forward in his chair, anxious for an answer.

Zimmerman decided to ignore the queasiness in his stomach and plunge right into the deep water that he knew lay ahead. "Mr. Holland, we have reason to believe that your organization was involved in his death."

"Algonquin? That's impossible! How?"

"Not Algonquin, Mr. Holland," Zimmerman persisted. He rose to his feet and took a step toward the man he was interrogating. "Look, we both know that Algonquin is nothing but a front for your other activities."

"Such as?" Holland asked, a flinty glint in his eyes.

"Where shall we begin? Bookmaking? Prostitution? Narcotics?" Zimmerman offered in challenge.

Holland stared silently at the policeman for a moment. Then he, too, rose to his feet. The two men stood, staring each other down, less than two feet from each other.

Finally, Holland spoke. In a choked, barely controlled voice, he commanded, "I think you'd better leave, Lieutenant. I believe this interview has ended."

"I'm not going anywhere until I've gotten some answers."

Holland regarded Zimmerman coolly as his control returned.

"Lieutenant Zimmerman, I can't imagine who has been telling you these ridiculous things, but I can assure you that neither I nor any of the Algonquin enterprises have anything to do with such nefarious activities. In short, sir, you're barking up the wrong tree."

"I don't think so, sir."

"I'm beginning to lose patience, Lieutenant. What you are alleging is patently untrue. Unless you have some kind of proof you'd like to offer, I suggest you leave before you force me to place a certain phone call that will put an end to this nonsense in a way I'm sure you'll find unpleasant. While I would hardly say that Commissioner Halloran and I are close friends, we do serve together on a variety of committees and civic-betterment boards."

"Go right ahead." Zimmerman called the bluff. "Phone anyone you please. My badge number is 303097."

Holland moved toward the telephone resting on a three-legged candlestand across the room. He paused when his hand came to rest on the receiver and looked into Zimmerman's eyes once more. All he saw was mild amusement.

"What is it you want, Lieutenant?" he half pleaded as his hand moved away from the phone. "You can't possibly tie any of those crimes you mentioned to me, or to my company. It's impossible. The ties don't exist. We have nothing to do with such things. Are you really so anxious to lose your badge? This is the craziest thing I've ever heard!"

"Let me worry about my badge, Mr. Holland. I just want some explanations. Particularly an explanation of the circumstances surrounding my brother's murder."

"Lieutenant, Lieutenant, I've already told you that I don't know anything about that. How could I?"

Zimmerman decided to play his one piece of trump.

"You could because you should. After all, you're the boss, Mr. Olanda."

Holland's composure deserted him completely. Panic lined his face and his eyes gleamed like those of a cornered bobcat.

"Wha— What? What did you call me?" he asked, obviously unwilling to believe that anybody could be resurrecting an identity that had been dead so long.

"Olanda, Thomas. Born, Brooklyn, 1912. Disappeared with no trace in 1935. Reappeared as Thomas Holland in Cincinnati that same year. Sound familiar?"

"I don't know what you're talking about," Holland spat.

"It's easy enough to prove, Mr. Olanda. A set of Olanda's fingerprints is still on file, you know, on an application for a handgun permit made back in 1933. As I recall, you were in charge of payroll for Dobler Trucking at the time, and you said you needed a gun because you sometimes carried large amounts of cash. It would be easy enough to match those prints against your own. If they don't match, you won't have to call the Commissioner—I'll hand you my badge."

While Zimmerman had been talking, Holland had been thinking.

"This Olanda, he didn't do anything wrong," Holland stated positively. "Even if you could prove that I was Olanda, you have nothing to charge either of us with."

"Sure I do." Zimmerman smiled. "How about draft evasion? World War Two, remember? An induction notice was sent to Thomas Olanda and returned "address unknown." And don't tell me that you're innocent because you never got the notice and didn't know you were being drafted. If you read the Selective Service Act, which I have done, you'll see that you have an obligation to keep your local board informed of any change of address. It's your responsibility to tell them when you move, and it's your neck if you don't."

"Lieutenant," Holland began, smiling in mock amusement, "you're way off base. I, Thomas Holland, I repeat—Holland—duly registered for the draft as required by law in 1940. I can probably dig up the exact date if I have to. In Cincinnati, Ohio, my place of birth. I can prove that, too. I was called for induction in 1943, as I recall, and I was exempted because I worked in a defense industry, that being Independent Products, Incorporated, in Detroit. My civilian work was considered vital to the war effort. All this can be verified, of course."

Holland rose and started toward the door. "Now, if that's all you wanted to discuss, I think you should leave. You have, quite frankly, wasted enough of my time already."

Zimmerman did not move.

"Mr. Holland, it would be very easy to establish whether or not you are Olanda. We can check fingerprints, as I said. After all, you have to appreciate my position. During the war, there was a thriving business in forged draft cards as well as phony birth certificates, passports, and other credentials. Deserters, refugees, draft dodgers—they all needed documents. Why don't the two of us take a ride over to my headquarters, where we can have you fingerprinted? Then we'll be able to either lay this whole business to rest or pursue it further. If you're not Olanda, you shouldn't have anything to hide."

Holland grimaced. "Oh, the logic of a cop! If you didn't do it, you have nothing to hide, indeed. I'm sorry, Lieutenant, my mind doesn't work that way. Now, I have been very patient with you and I've given you considerably more time than you deserve. I certainly don't have any more time to waste on you and I'm not about to go with you now or any other time. If you want to bring me to police headquarters,

114

I'd suggest you get a warrant for my arrest, if, of course, you can trump up some charge. I know my rights, though, Lieutenant, and I can assure you I'll exercise them to the fullest. False-arrest suits can be very costly, you know, and my lawyers are among the best in the country."

"You'll have to prove malice, Mr. Holland, if you want a false-arrest charge to stick. And you can't. I do have reasonable cause to bring Olanda in, and I believe you are Olanda."

"What reasonable cause? You still haven't told me anything that this Olanda has done wrong."

"Yes, I did. Draft evasion."

"If I was Olanda, I could get off that charge. I did register for the draft."

". . . And then there's fraud."

Holland had regained much of his confidence after the earlier onslaught, but this new composure fled with equal dispatch.

"Fraud?"

"Right. Olanda had a Social Security card, and so do you. That's two accounts. If you are one and the same man, that represents intent to commit fraud by filing two claims and collecting twice. Also, Holland may have registered for the draft and found a cop-out, but Olanda never answered the call. Believe me, Mr. Holland, we can make quite a lot of trouble for you if we choose to do so. Even if you got off on all charges, I don't think the stockholders of the Algonquin Corporation are going to care for the publicity their president is attracting."

"But that's blackmail, Lieutenant!"

Zimmerman looked at Holland with determination. "Why, did you think you guys had a monopoly on dirty playing? Let me make one thing abundantly clear, sir; I will do whatever I have to do to get the information I want."

Holland relaxed as he gave in to the situation that confronted him. His eyes examined the fine weave of the rug and he asked, "What is it you want to know? I'm not admitting anything, you understand. I am not this Olanda person, nor have I ever heard of him. But you seem determined to make as much fuss as you can if you don't get what you want. I don't know what I can do for you, but I might know some people—one hears that this man or that is involved in things—and I might be able to help you. I'd be willing to try, under the condition that you cease this harassment."

"Find out," Zimmerman ordered. "I want to know who killed my brother and why. I want to know why the body of Daniel DiBennidetto was left on my doorstep the other night. And while you're at it, I want to know what this gang war is all about. That should be enough for starters."

Holland nodded in acquiescence. "You'll find some magazines in the desk drawer. I'll be back in a few moments." He turned on his heel and disappeared from the room, treading a little more heavily than when he had entered.

He was back before Zimmerman had finished the article he was reading about a 1968 Antarctic expedition in a *National Geographic* of similar vintage.

"Lieutenant," he began cautiously, "I want it clearly understood that you did not get any of this information from me. It could have repercussions, if you follow my meaning. Very unpleasant repercussions."

Zimmerman nodded in agreement.

"Well, as I just got the story, you brother was killed by this DiBennidetto person. Apparently there was some kind of misunderstanding about a gambling debt, and DiBennidetto got carried away in his efforts to collect. To make a long story short, his superiors did not approve of his actions, so they called DiBennidetto in and questioned him to ascertain the reasons for his extreme actions. DiBennidetto lied to them and swore that he had not done it. He did

116

indicate, by the way, that he had placed a call to the widow to see if her insurance money would cover the debt. Some people never give up, I suppose.

"At any rate, DiBennidetto named several of his cronies who supposedly were with him at the time of your brother's death. And as it happens, several of them belonged to a different faction of the Organization than did his employers.

"Now you must understand the psychology involved here, Lieutenant. These men are like medieval barons and princes. Borgias, Medicis, and that sort. As soon as they realized that one of their rank was involved with the warlord across the street, they started smelling a palace plot. A coup. They reacted accordingly, exactly as the Borgias might have done. That is what caused the many slayings that have recently taken place.

"You must remember—you did not get any of this information from me. You know how those people are. You have a great example of their methods right here in the events I have just described. You have placed me in considerable danger, you know, with your questions."

"Let me ask you this," Zimmerman questioned. "DiBennidetto must have known how his bosses would react if he told them he was hanging around with the competition? Why did he admit it to them?"

"Yes. I asked the same question," Holland replied. "My sources told me, and I quote, 'There are ways to get information.' I'll ask you, Lieutenant: was DiBennidetto tortured?"

Zimmerman nodded his head affirmatively.

"I see." He shuddered. "And we call this world civilized!"

"One thing still isn't too clear, if you'll bear with me," Zimmerman said. "Why did DiBennidetto lie to them in the first place? They might have punished him for being overzealous if he went too far in collecting a debt. But surely they wouldn't have killed him?"

117

"Who knows, Lieutenant? I did ask about that, and the response I got confirmed your feelings. If he had just told them the truth, they might not have trusted his judgment for a while, but in all likelihood, he would still be alive. The only thing I can suggest is that DiBennidetto was none too bright and he panicked. That would seem to give a reason for his call to the widow—he was instructed to collect the debt, not murder a man. Perhaps he felt that if he could succeed in getting the money, they would be more likely to forgive his earlier indiscretion.

"No, the one thing that the Organization will simply not tolerate is a man whom they cannot trust. Having lied to them was far the worse sin than having killed your brother."

Zimmerman toyed with the idea of continuing his interrogation until Holland revealed the identities of his sources. Such information could have future uses. But he decided, at length, that Holland would probably not reveal them no matter how hard he pushed. People were getting murdered, and Holland had already indicated that he had well-founded fears about joining their ranks.

"Thank you, Mr. Holland," the policeman said as he headed for the door to the street. "You've been very helpful."

"You won't say where the information came from . . . ?" Holland implored but Zimmerman was out on the street before he had to answer.

Remembering something that had not occurred to him earlier, Zimmerman turned back and pulled the door chime once more. This time, Holland answered the door himself.

"Yes, Lieutenant?"

"One thing you still haven't explained. Why was DiBennidetto's body delivered to me? You've explained all the internal politics that led up to the warfare, but I still don't understand how *I* fit in."

Holland shrugged. "That, I am told, should be construed

by you as a peace offering. An apology, if you will," he explained. "Let's face it, the last thing these people want is to get a police lieutenant angry with them if they can avoid it. What they were telling you in their unique way was 'Here is your brother's killer, you need look no further. What's more, he has already been punished.' "

Zimmerman was morbidly impressed with the gravity of the "apology," but it seemed to make sense, so he accepted the explanation. Turning back to the street, he glanced over and saw a uniformed patrolman inspecting his automobile. The officer had already removed his pad of parking citations and was thumbing to a blank page.

"Hey, wait a minute," Zimmerman called to him as he sized up the traffic quickly and darted across the street. "Didn't you see my police identification?"

"Your what?" the policeman asked.

Zimmerman glanced at the windshield and saw that his card had, indeed, been removed from view. Opening the door, he reached in and flipped the sun visor down so that it was once again displayed.

"Well, Christ," the patrolman exclaimed. "How the hell am I supposed to know you're on the force when you keep it hidden?" Mumbling to himself, he ripped the ticket he had started from his pad and shoved it into his back pocket. "I've got to account for this number, you know," he informed Zimmerman in annoyance. "These citations are numbered in order and when I get back to the station house tonight, my sergeant is going to ask what happened to 719496. Then I'm going to have to tell him what happened, and he's going to give me two forms to fill out in triplicate. With luck, you've only made me a half hour late for dinner tonight."

"Sorry, officer," Zimmerman said. "I could have sworn I displayed it when I left the car. I guess I forgot." He shrugged his shoulders.

"Sure. Do me a favor, though. Next time make sure, will you?"

Zimmerman got into the car, glanced quickly at the street behind him, and pulled out into traffic. Holland's explanation ran through his mind as he automatically made the correct turns. He was not really conscious of driving until he was on the approach ramp to the Brooklyn-Battery Tunnel which would take him back to Manhattan and his office. He pulled up to the toll booth, having searched in vain through his pockets for the appropriate change, and handed the collector a five-dollar bill. This earned him not his first dirty look of the day.

Stuffing the paper and silver change in his hip pocket to be sorted out later, he quickly accelerated into the merging traffic entering the tunnel. He had to hit his brakes almost as quickly as he came abreast of the cars, which were funneling into a single lane. This was the only tube open today, due to repairs on the others, and it carried one lane of cars in each direction, to and from Manhattan. Somewhere on my desk, he mused, there is a report telling us to avoid the tunnel today; that it is under repair. Someday, perhaps I'll have the time to read it.

Entering the tunnel, he blinked as his eyes adjusted to the different light. He quickly rolled up his window as the first exhaust fumes assaulted his nostrils. Two-way traffic flowed on the tube's two lanes, and he felt the rush of wind as other automobiles passed in the opposite direction. He had never driven through the tunnel with traffic flowing in both directions before—normally, alternate tubes carried cars each way—and he became increasingly conscious of the narrowness of the lanes as the traffic on the opposite lane seemed to be heading at him on a collision course.

Zimmerman never actually had a chance to acknowledge the fact that his car was out of control. One moment he was cruising along at forty miles an hour following the car in front of him, and next thing he knew his car had just scraped the side wall of the roadway. When he tried to steer out into the center of the lane again, carefully turning the wheel so as not to send his vehicle into the path of the oncoming traffic, he found that the car did not respond. More boldly now, he cut the wheel sharply to his left. In naval parlance, it was not answering the helm. Disregarding the truck that rode ominously close to his rear bumper, he slammed his right foot on the brake. His spirits lifted as the brakes grabbed, but fell just as quickly when his foot continued its descent until the face of the pedal was almost flush with the floorboard.

Thinking quickly, he tried to down-shift the car to a halt. As he went from drive down into second gear, the transmission protested, but did slow the car to about twenty-five miles an hour. Encouraged by his success, he shifted speedily down to low. Whirring and whining, the car rejected this selection and chose instead to jerk forward with a jolt that bounced it once more off the retaining wall. Sparks showered back as the right fender scraped the reinforced concrete. This, at least, had a positive effect—the truck behind Zimmerman's car slowed to widen the gap between them. The truck driver flashed his lights on and off in warning. Although Zimmerman had removed his foot from the gas pedal, the car now began to accelerate as the tunnel sloped downhill. The pitch was so slight that he had never before noticed the tunnel was not perfectly level, yet it sent the car closer and closer to the car it followed.

"Oh my God," Zimmerman thought as he recalled that a few hundred yards ahead the tunnel turned. Somehow one always thought of underwater passages like this as being perfectly straight. Yet, whether to avoid rock in the bed of the bay or for some other reason, this one was not.

His car was out of control, but his mind was not. As soon

as he realized that a collision of some sort was inevitable, he made up his mind to minimize the risks. Reaching under the dashboard, he flicked the toggle switch that activated the car's emergency blinker lights. In the same motion, he punched the button that turned on the siren he had had installed to facilitate his getting to his office or to a crime scene quickly should he have to do so. The sound, confined to the narrow tube of the tunnel walls, was deafening. As he climbed to his knees on the front seat and vaulted over into the rear of the car, he saw the cars around him reacting uncertainly. The truck that had been tailing him had slowed to almost a complete halt, while the driver ahead seemed on the verge of panic, erratically hitting his brakes and speeding up, not sure what to do.

Zimmerman squeezed his frame sideways on the floor between the back seat and the back of the front seat, facing backward. He began to count seconds as he awaited the crash. One thousand and one, one thousand and two . . . The impact came just as he had finished saying one thousand and eight. When the car reached the curve, it struck the unyielding side wall with a metal-rending crunch, the tail end swung out on the carom, slamming into an oncoming car in the opposite lane. Zimmerman had prepared himself for this, but he was not ready for the magnitude of the sound. His ears were still ringing when, assured that the vehicle had finally come to rest, he rose from his cramped position and looked around.

Reaching forward, he leaned across the front seat and pushed the button to silence his siren. The sound died, decreasing in pitch like the air going out of a balloon. The rear door on the driver's side was completely blocked by the smashed front end of the car he had struck. The other door still worked, however, so he left that way. As he crawled out, a shower of glass fragments fell from his head and jacket, tinkling as they rained down on the ground.

The driver of the other car was also emerging onto the roadway. The man was visibly shaken.

"Are you all right?" Zimmerman asked, displaying his badge. "My steering and brakes went. Didn't you hear the siren or see my lights?"

"They were coming the other way. Jesus, you crossed right over into my lane and hit me! You could have killed me."

"Are you all right?" Zimmerman asked again. "Would you like me to get medical assistance for you?"

"Look at that car! I made the last payment on it two months ago, and just look at it now. It's a wreck. A total wreck!"

"Well, there's nothing wrong with your voice," Zimmerman said sarcastically. "Now I'll ask once more—would you like me to try to get medical assistance for you?"

The man looked at Zimmerman tensely as he regained his composure. "No," he finally answered. "I think I'm all right."

Behind them, cars out of view of the wreckage began blowing their horns impatiently. "Cut that out, you idiot," shouted one driver who could see what had happened. "There's been an accident."

"So what am I supposed to do?" came an answering shout. "Sit here all day?" The horn-blowing started up again.

While he waited for the tow truck, Zimmerman's policeman's mind began to analyze the accident. Steering could always fail, he supposed. And brakes could always fail. But for the two vital systems to go out of commission simultaneously was a little too much of a coincidence for him to accept. Particularly when dealing with the Organization.

CHAPTER 20

"WHO'S IN CHARGE of Brooklyn North Patrol these days?" Lieutenant Zimmerman demanded of anybody who happened to be in earshot as he stomped into the offices of Manhattan Homicide South.

"Patrol?" asked Detective Third Class Peter Thompson, looking up from his desk. "Don't you mean detectives? That's Captain Barringer and Lieutenant Kohlmar. You know them. . . ."

"I said Patrol and I meant Patrol. Brooklyn North. You remember Patrol," he added sarcastically. "The fellows in the blue suits with the badges on the front?"

The detectives looked at each other to see if anyone knew. Bob Slocum, one of the newer detectives, who had himself been in uniform just eight months ago, finally volunteered: "It used to be Captain Osgood. I think his first name is Tom or Ted or something. I don't know if he's still there, though . . ."

No sooner had Slocum mentioned the name than Zimmerman's mind flashed an image of the man. A hard-working, stolid man, Osgood seemed ideally suited for his job. There are two schools of thought: one, that a good administrator can administer anything; the other, that the man in charge should be thoroughly familiar with every job under his command. Osgood was that latter type. His career had begun almost thirty years ago, pounding a beat in Brownsville. When he had mastered that, he was put on black-and-white patrol-car duty. He had attacked that assignment with characteristic vigilance and in time gained his sergeant's stripes. The big promotion, the one in which he made lieutenant, had occurred several years later. Osgood had made a habit of taking examinations for promotion as soon as his time in grade was sufficient to meet the qualification requirements. Then he waited. When an opening presented itself, he hoped to himself that it would be his chance, but he never said anything to anyone else. Sooner or later, it would be his turn.

The distinguishing thing about Osgood's career was that, as an individual, he had never particularly distinguished himself. He had always mastered whatever job he was given to do, and a review of his performance always indicated that the work had been done extremely well and with a minimum of fuss. Yet he had never received any citations for valor or heroism, and he had never been wounded in the line of duty. He could probably count the times he had fired his gun—not including the mandatory sessions on the firing range—on the fingers of both bands. Osgood was to his type of police work what Joe DiMaggio was to playing the outfield. No sensational catches—he made them all look easy. In short, he was the consummate professional.

Osgood answered the phone on the second ring.

"Tom? This is Al Zimmerman over in Manhattan South Homicide. I want to know who you had on foot patrol on the twenty-one-hundred block on Hicks Street at about nine forty-five this morning."

"We don't run too many foot patrols over there anymore," the ruddy-faced captain replied. "It's a residential area, and we usually patrol it in black-and-whites. Foot patrols are only used these days in commercial areas, shopping streets and suchlike. Why do you ask?"

"I ran into a guy on foot over there this morning. Mid-fifties, gray hair, sort of beefy. I'm trying to find out who he was."

"What's the matter, Al, didn't he salute when you passed?" The friction between patrol officers and detectives began to come out.

"No, Tom. I think he tried to kill me."

"What?" Osgood demanded. Zimmerman related his activities from the time he left Hicks Street to his disastrous journey through the tunnel.

"The car had to have been tampered with, Tom. For the brakes and steering to have failed at the same time, there's simply no other explanation."

Osgood had said no more than "MmHmmn" while Zimmerman had told his the story. Now, when Zimmerman paused, it was his turn.

"What were you doing over in our neck of the woods, anyway?" he asked.

"That has nothing to do with it," Zimmerman said, irritated. "Now would you please check your roster and see who was there at that time? About a quarter to ten this morning."

"Sure, Al, sure. Don't get hot under the collar."

"I'm sorry if I seem impatient, Tom. But somebody did try to kill me. I'm just trying to find out who it was."

"Okay. I understand. Can you hold on a minute? I'll get the duty sheets."

The lieutenant drummed his fingers impatiently on his desk as he waited for the captain to return to the phone. About two minutes later, Osgood's voice again sounded in his ear.

"I don't know who it could have been, Al. We definitely didn't have anybody on foot there this morning. I didn't think we had, and the duty sheets bear it out. Car three-o-six passed there at about ten-o-five, though. I radioed to them, and they say that they've been cruising all morning. The only time they got out of their car was for a coffee break about fifteen minutes ago. I believe them, too. They're both

126

good men—Impellitieri and Foster. One's about five-foot-eight and swarthy; the other's a black man. Those are the only two men I've had anywhere near there so far today. They don't sound anything like the guy you're talking about. It sounds like you met up with a ringer—somebody impersonating an officer. If he tried to kill you, I sure hope it wasn't one of my men. But I don't see how it could have been, to tell you the truth."

Zimmerman heard Osgood talking to someone away from the telephone.

"Al," Osgood said when he returned to his conversation with Zimmerman, "is there anything else I can do for you? We're sort of busy around here this morning."

"No, Tom. You confirmed what I already suspected."

"Good. Anything else you need, just give me a call. And by the way," he added in closing, "thanks for calling this to my attention. If there's a ringer wandering around in our district, I'll tell the boys in the cars to keep their eyes open for him. Who knows, we might get lucky."

"Sure. Thanks, Tom, "Zimmerman said as he hung up. Both policemen knew that the odds against the imposter popping up again in uniform anywhere near the place he originally appeared were very slim indeed.

CHAPTER 21

"WELL, WHERE DO I go from here?" Al Zimmerman asked Bon Donofrio as the sergeant drove him home that evening. He had spent the remainder of the day in the Records section looking for a face that matched the pseudo-policeman. He had first queried the computerized identification system for all men over forty with arrest records for impersonating an officer, and who were not now in prison. The resulting print-out had referred him to forty-two files. It had taken slightly over an hour just to pull them. He was able to run through the pictures they contained in half that time. There were no familiar faces.

His next step had been to instruct the computer to give him the names of all the men in its memory bank that had both affiliations with organized crime and a record of training, employment, or modus operandi that indicated knowledgeability of the internal working of automobiles. This list was much longer, containing one hundred and seventy-three names. As he began pulling these files, he saw that the second one he looked at included the note that the man was now serving a term at the Green Haven Correctional Institution in Stormville. Grumbling, he remembered that he had not told the computer to eliminate prisoners on this go-around. Thus, he had to return to the computer and ask it the same questions again, this time with the missing stipulation.

The list now was reduced to sixty-seven possibilities. By

the time he had shuffled through these files, his eyes felt as if they were on fire, and a throbbing headache had begun to creep from his temples across his brow. There was still no sign of the man he had met that morning. The thought crossed his mind that the offender could have been a genuine policeman, despite Captain Osgood's denial. But the job of sifting through personnel files to dig out photographs of all the men in Osgood's command was too staggering for him to contemplate. That's a last resort, he thought, dreading the task should it actually become necessary.

Seated beside his friend Donofrio in the car, he rubbed his eyes and silently hoped that he would be able to get a good night's sleep.

"What's the problem, Al?" Donofrio asked in response to Zimmerman's earlier inquiry. "I thought the case was solved. DiBennidetto killed your brother. Holland told you that."

"Sure he did. And then he tried to have me killed."

Donofrio had stopped for a red light, and he took the occasion to look over at his weary friend. "What makes you so sure it was Holland? After all, he told you that there were some rival factions at work. My guess was that it was one of them."

"Maybe you're right, Bob. Or else Holland told me as much as he did because he felt that I wouldn't live long enough to do anything about it."

A horn hooted behind Donofrio's car, causing the sergeant to return his full attention to the road.

"Could be," Donofrio admitted. "Or else you might have really scared him when you tied him to Olanda. Maybe we ought to take a closer look at that. I wonder if Mr. Holland's affairs could stand really close scrutiny. Particularly at about the time he changed his name. I'm sure he's aware that there isn't any statute of limitations on fraud, and he was, or I should say is, a businessman. Maybe you and I ought to get our magnifying glasses and take a real look."

"No," Zimmerman said emphatically.

"Why not?"

"Not our territory. He's in Brooklyn North, remember?"

Donofrio shook his head from side to side in disbelief. "Al, sometimes I don't understand you at all."

"Bob, let me put it like this— I know that I'm overstepping my bounds when I start nosing around in Brooklyn in investigating my brother's death. It's beyond my jurisdiction. I'd be pretty stupid if I didn't realize that; I've been reminded often enough. Now it's one thing when I violate procedure to try to find the facts behind what happened to my brother. It's something else entirely when I begin to investigate everything that's going on in Brooklyn. In other words, I can only carry this investigation so far and no further. McIlhenny is nervous because I'm doing spadework in somebody else's backyard. Can you imagine how he'd react if he found out that I was digging into things that aren't directly related to my brother's murder? He'd land on me with both feet, and rightly so."

"Hmmm," Donofrio more or less agreed. "In that case, Al, what's the problem? I mean, you know who killed your brother. If that's all your pursuing, then the case should be closed. You've got the answer."

"I've got *an* answer, Bob. That doesn't mean I believe it."

"Oh, for God's sake!" Donofrio exclaimed in exasperation. "The man who, as close as any of us can tell, is the head of the Organization locally, told you that Di-Bennidetto killed your brother. He told you why. Then, to wrap things up into a nice, neat package, he took care of punishing the killer. What more could he do? Swear out an affidavit? The Organization even made an attempt on your life because you knew too much about their internal workings. What more do you want?"

"I don't know. Maybe it's just too pat. Maybe there are still too many questions that need answers before I can accept that story."

"Like what?"

"Like the fact that disloyalty is the worst sin that a member of the Syndicate can commit, yet DiBennidetto committed it without a second thought. That's why they killed him, after all. For lying to them about having killed my brother. Not for having killed him. Oh, the fact that they believed him to have been my brother's assassin was the reason for them depositing him on my doorstep, all right. But the reason they killed him was that he refused to admit he had done it. He kept insisting that he hadn't. If he had admitted to his bosses that he had, in fact, committed the murder, they would have punished him, no doubt, but they wouldn't have killed him.

"Now the significant thing here is that DiBennidetto knew this. He knew he could have saved his own life if he had confessed to them. Yet he didn't. I don't know what that tells you, but to me it says that there's a reasonably good chance that he didn't do it. It's my opinion that loyalty to his bosses was so deeply ingrained in him that he couldn't bring himself to lie to them and say he had killed my brother, even though he knew that that lie could save his life. What I'm saying is that I don't think he did it."

"Whew," Donofrio said after digesting this for a moment. "That leaves one big question, though, doesn't it? If DiBennidetto didn't kill your brother, who did?"

For the balance of the trip, neither man spoke, each deep in thought as he pondered that question.

CHAPTER 22

THE NEXT MORNING, Lieutenant Zimmerman had to take a taxi to work. In that he had parking space available to him at his office, he had not made proximity to a subway station a prerequisite in selecting his apartment years before, and his home was a thirty-minute walk from the nearest rapid-transit point. Grudgingly handing the driver a five-dollar bill to cover the fare, he opened the door and crawled out of the cramped cab. He ignored the driver's sarcasm at the thirty-cent tip, and as he straightened up on the sidewalk, he checked his wallet, noting regretfully that its remaining cash contents were limited to a single dollar bill, with which he would have to purchase his lunch and get himself home that evening. Shaking his head sadly, he resigned himself to having to beg a ride from Donofrio again.

Zimmerman was so wrapped up in these thoughts that he didn't see Lieutenant Snyder getting out of a patrol car directly behind his cab.

"Al Zimmerman, just the man I wanted to see" Snyder called after him as he started ascending the steps. He turned quickly and faced the other lieutenant.

"Duke. Hi." He paused and allowed Snyder to catch up with him. The two men continued on into the police headquarters building together. "What brings you out here? Have you decided finally to come over and see how the other half lives?"

"No, as a matter of fact, I really did come here to see you. Actually, I wanted to see what it was about this building that made you prefer my side of the East River."

"Huh?"

"Well," Snyder continued, a definite edge in his voice, "you seem to want to spend most of your time over in my bailiwick, so I thought I'd drop by and see if they needed a good homicide lieutenant over here."

The two men continued up the interior stairs and into Zimmerman's office.

"You want some coffee?" the host lieutenant offered.

"No, I didn't come here for coffee, Al. I want to know what you were doing in Brooklyn yesterday, and what, if anything, you found out."

Zimmerman regarded Snyder coolly. "I don't suppose you'd believe me if I said I was over there to see my sister-in-law?"

"No, I wouldn't. Her house is more than eight miles from Hicks Street."

Zimmerman reached into his desk and withdrew two coffee cups.

"You're sure?" he asked, gesturing with the cups.

"Oh all right. Black."

Zimmerman left the office to go to the coffeepot in the squad room. He returned a moment later, placing one cup on his desk and handing the other to his guest. "Careful, it's hot," he warned.

"How did you hear that I was in Brooklyn yesterday?"

"We *do* talk to each other, you know. I had a call from Osgood as soon as he got off the phone with you. We may not have the glamour of you hotshots in Manhattan, but we do try to keep each other informed. Which is more than I can say for some cops I can think of."

"Okay, Duke. You've made your point. I was going to call you this morning anyway and fill you in."

"Sure you were," Snyder said disbelievingly.

For the next twenty minutes, Zimmerman outlined exactly what had happened the previous day, from the interview with Holland to the attempt on his life. Snyder listened patiently, without interrupting. Only occasionally did his face show any sign of surprise at what Zimmerman was revealing.

Snyder did not speak until he was sure that Zimmerman had completed his narrative.

"So you went out and bearded Holland in his den," he said, a tremor in his voice betraying the fury he contained. "Let me ask you, Al. Did it ever occur to you that we might have been watching Holland for other reasons? Reasons a lot more important than one murder?"

Zimmerman shrugged his shoulders helplessly.

"We've known about this Holland-Orlanda business for a long time. We've been waiting for the right time to use it. In fact, we've been working very closely with the organized crime unit of the D.A.'s office trying to build a case that would put the elegant Mr. Holland behind bars for the rest of his life. You blew that, didn't you?"

Zimmerman sighed. Then, struck by another thought, he reached for the phone and asked the switchboard operator for Bernie Majelewski, Manhattan South's captain in charge of Patrol. Snyder sat dumbstruck at his colleague's rudeness.

"Bernie," Zimmerman asked when the captain completed the connection, "let me ask you something. If a guy, one of your guys, has to void a parking ticket, how does he do it? How does he account for that numbered chit?"

Zimmerman appeared relieved as he hung up. "That's what I thought," he announced. "He just turns in the voided ticket. He doesn't have to fill out any forms at all."

He looked Snyder in the eye. "You know what that means, don't you? The guy who tampered with my car wasn't a cop, after all. He was a phony." He paused and smiled into Snyder's disbelieving face. "I had this horrible thought that I was going to have to look at all the pictures on all the police personnel files in the city."

Snyder allowed his rage to show through. Rising, he leaned across Zimmerman's desk and barked, "You haven't heard a word I've said, have you? You're going right ahead with your investigation!" He stared at the offender, not knowing what to say next. The men looked at each other speechlessly, Zimmerman smiling while Snyder glared. Finally, Snyder straightened up and regained control of himself. "Al," he said in a calmer voice, "I'll just say this. If I ever hear that you've been seen in my territory again, if I ever even suspect that you're still after Holland, I'm going to make a formal complaint to the Chief of Detectives. You've invested a lot of time in your career as a cop, so I don't want to do that. So stay out of my way!"

He wheeled about on his heel in a perfectly executed about-face and stormed out of the room, slamming the door behind him so that glass rattled and Zimmerman's coffee sloshed over the lip of his cup.

Seated behind his desk, Zimmerman was still smiling. He had been honestly afraid that the man who had doctored his car had been a genuine policeman, and not only would that have meant endless searching through records to establish the man's identity, it would have been a black mark on the Department.

When the smile faded, he reached into his IN basket and took the first file off the top. He was pleased to note that it related to the Dunway case.

CHAPTER 23

ZIMMERMAN HAD MANAGED to concentrate on the Dunway case for over an hour before his thoughts drifted back to his brother. It was not until he realized that he was reading the same page for the third time without digesting its contents that he put the paper down. Rubbing his eyes with his stubby fingers, he sat back in his chair and wondered whether another cup of coffee might help.

Before he could decide, the phone rang.

"Lieutenant Zimmerman?" asked the vaguely familiar voice at the other end.

"Yes?"

"This is Sergeant Kroning down on the gun range, sir. I've been going through the records, and according to my sheet, you haven't done your qualifying rounds for this year yet. I tried to call you a few weeks ago, but they said you were on vacation. Didn't you get a message?"

"No, Kroning, I didn't."

"Well sir, you know you have to requalify every year. Is it possible that you already did, but somehow it didn't get into the records? You have to file a qualification form that I countersign, you know. Some of the fellows forget."

Zimmerman considered briefly the alternative of lying to Kroning and telling him that he had taken the tests but had neglected to file the form. Oh, he's only doing his job, he decided, and chose to admit the truth.

"No, Sergeant. I haven't qualified this year yet. To tell

you the truth, I've just been too busy to get down there and take care of it. How about next week sometime? Toward the end of the week would be best for me."

"I'm sorry sir, but you're already overdue. Unless you're qualified by the end of this week, the rules say I'll have to file a delinquency report. I'm sorry sir, but those are the rules."

"Look, Kroning, I appreciate that you have a job to do and you're only trying to do it, but I'm really up to my ears in work. Couldn't you hold off till next week? You know how it is."

"I'd like to help you out, Lieutenant. But rules are rules. If I made an exception for you, then I'd have to make exceptions for everybody. You can see that, can't you, sir?"

"Okay, okay." Zimmerman looked at his wristwatch. "How about now? I might as well get it over with. I can be down there in about five minutes." Zimmerman knew himself. If he didn't go through the procedure immediately, he would put it off again with some other excuse till next week. In that light, it was better to do it now and not have it hanging over him as another piece of bureaucracy that had to be dealt with before he could forget about it for another year.

"Yes, sir. As it happens, there is a spot open on the range now. Make it soon, though, will you, sir? The whole range is booked for the rest of the day, starting in about an hour."

For the number of times he had to fire his gun in the course of his actual work, all this practice seemed excessive, Zimmerman thought as he rode down in the elevator to the basement firing range. The way each shot fired had to be accounted for with what seemed like reams of paperwork in triplicate was the soundest assurance that no policeman was going to get trigger-happy.

Arriving at the soundproofed underground hallway that served as a gun range, Zimmerman signed in with the sergeant and drew his targets and ammunition. "Remember, Lieutenant," Kroning said, "you can have six practice shots for a group in each position. Then they count. If you want to use one of your practice targets," he allowed, "I'll let you. It better be good, though."

Circling carefully around the backs of the other men on the firing range, Zimmerman took up the last position in the line. The gunfire around him set up a din that set him to wondering how Kroning could stand spending his life down here. As he wheeled the target holder toward him, using an apparatus like a clothesline with a crank, Zimmerman considered the fact that Kroning was probably deaf enough by now not to be bothered by the noise. Something like boilermaker's syndrome of selective deafness in certain frequency ranges, he supposed.

He clipped his first target to the spring clamp and sent it back to its position against the bullet-absorbent backdrop. He removed his side arm from its holster, emptied the shells from their cylinders and dropped them in his trouser pocket. When the gun was empty, he refilled it with the ammunition that the sergeant had issued him. Carefully, he maneuvered his body and feet into the correct "standing" position, facing the side wall and looking down the gun barrel as it extended in precisely parallel-to-the-ground fashion—an extension of the straight line formed by his right arm and hand. He tightened his index finger slowly, with the prescribed even pressure he had learned at the police academy. The first shot exploded forth exactly as it should—while he was still applying pressure evenly to the trigger.

The jolt of the explosion sent his hand and arm approximately six inches up. Quickly, but with precision, he lowered them back on target and squeezed off another shot. This procedure was repeated four more times before he placed the pistol on the table beside him and wheeled in the target.

As he inspected the one-and-a-half-inch cluster in which the bullet holes had torn through the heart of the man-shaped silhouette on the paper, he rubbed his right wrist where the kick of the gun had concentrated its impact.

Pleased with his work and not wanting to waste any more time than he had to, he signaled Kroning to come over and certify the target. While the sergeant inspected the entry and affixed his signature as a witness, Zimmerman fixed another silhouette onto the frame and cranked it out.

Sinking to one knee, the Lieutenant cracked out six more shots with similar dispatch. The results were equally positive.

Zimmerman had been annoyed at the nuisance of having to waste time on the firing range when he had so many other things to do; but when he had finished, he felt a tinge of pride at having done so well with so little practice. It was not until he reloaded his gun with his own ammunition and moved to replace it in its holster that he realized how sore his wrist was. I must be getting old and arthritic, he thought as he rubbed the wrist on his way up in the elevator. I'll stick to this .38 police special, though. Many of the younger policemen favored the more powerful .357 magnum. He had fired the magnum once, a few years back, when it had been first allowed as an acceptable alternate for policemen. It had taken almost a week before the vestiges of the pain in his hand and wrist had ceased.

The time on the range had done him good, he decided, when he found himself tackling the files in front of him with renewed vigor. Whatever the reason, it had cleared his head. That afternoon, he slashed through the paperwork like a snowplow clearing a road.

CHAPTER 24

"WHAT'S THE MATTER with your hand?" Kathy Zimmerman asked her husband as they were having dinner that evening.

"Firing range," he answered perfunctorily. "I guess I'm not as young as I used to be." He manipulated his wrist to work off the soreness.

"You know," he said, changing the subject, "I'm going to have to do something about a car. Bob drove me home again tonight. I'm not going to be able to ask him to play chauffeur forever. It's quite a bit out of his way."

"What does the insurance company say?" Kathy asked. "When will they give us a check?"

"I hate to tell you," he admitted, "but I haven't really spoken to them yet. Oh, I called Bill Hirshfeld yesterday after the accident and told him what had happened, that the car had been wrecked and all. Needless to say, I didn't tell him that I think the car was tampered with. But after all, he's just the insurance salesman, not the adjuster. He said he'd send some forms for me to fill out. Did we get get any mail from him today?"

"No. The way the mails are, they'll probably get here next week sometime."

"Yeah. Well, I don't know whether I ought to rent a car, or what. The subway is too far, and cabs cost a fortune."

"Car rentals aren't exactly cheap, you know. I don't

know what you're going to use for money. Doesn't the insurance cover that—a car rental while the other is being fixed or replaced?"

"I don't know," he answered. "Maybe I'll call Hirshfeld again tomorrow and find out. That's a good idea. The insurance should pay for that. After all, it's a legitimate expense."

Kathy had just got up to clear away the plates while he sipped at a cup of coffee when the doorbell rang.

"Sit down," she told him as he started to rise. "I'll get it."

He sank back in the chair and took another skimming sip at the steaming coffee as she disappeared from sight. He heard mumbled speech from the foyer but couldn't make out who was there or what was being said. He didn't really care. He was tired, and he only wished that his wife would get rid of the caller as soon as possible. The last thing he wanted was for a neighbor to drop in to pass the time. There was a night baseball game on television that started in less than half an hour, and he intended to watch it. If, that is, he could stay awake that long.

When he heard the door being shut, he expected to see his wife come back into the room. But not on the fly. She came through the doorway in a stumble-footed run, as if she had been shoved. He began to get up to help her, when a man's voice commanded: "Sit!"

Standing in the doorway was a beefy man in his early fifties. His mottled face and blue-lined, puffy nose showed signs of more than one bout with the bottle. At first, Zimmerman didn't recognize him. He looked different out of uniform.

"You . . ." Zimmerman began. "You're the cop who tried to ticket me yesterday."

The hulk smiled savagely, showing the brownest front teeth the lieutenant had ever seen. Both upper canines were missing. It was only when he took a step into the

141

room that Zimmerman saw that his right hand held a revolver.

"What do you want?" he asked. "I won't pretend that it's nice seeing you again."

"I have a message for you, Lieutenant," the man said. "Keep your nose out of what's none of your business."

"I see," Zimmerman said in calm rage. This was the same message that everyone, policeman and gangster alike, had been delivering to him in one way or another since his brother's death. "And could you tell me whose business I'm supposedly nosing around in this time?"

"Never you mind," the gunman growled. "Just butt out."

"Come on, come on," Zimmerman insisted. "Everybody and his brother has been telling me to say out of their business for some time now. If I don't know who I'm supposed to leave alone, how can I do it?"

Lines of concern furrowed the intruder's craggy face, giving it the appearance of a relief map of a mountain range. He had expected to be able to deliver his message and leave. Now that he was being told to make some decisions, he was unsure of himself.

"I can't tell you that," he protested. "He said you'd know." Panic crept into his eyes as he became aware of the fact that although he was holding the gun, he had lost the advantage. He began backing out. "I was told to deliver that message; I delivered that message. Keep your nose out of where it don't belong."

"Okay," Zimmerman called after him as he backed into the living room and began to fade from sight behind the partition that separated the two rooms, "I'll tell Holland next time I see him that you delivered the message."

The name quickly brought the intruder back into the room. "I never said anything about Mr. Holland," he protested. "I never told you who it was."

It was Zimmerman's turn to smile. "No, you didn't. And

142

when I see Holland, I'll be sure to tell him that you said the message wasn't from him."

"You can't do that," the man implored. "You're twisting everything I say. You're not *supposed* to see him anymore."

"Oh." Zimmerman chuckled fearsomely. "Then it *was* Holland who sent you."

"I didn't say that!" The gunman drew closer to Zimmerman and began waving the pistol in his face. For the first time, the thought crossed the detective's mind that he might be pushing this man just far enough to use the firearm. His peripheral vision told him that his wife was cowering in a corner of the room, some seven feet away—well out of the line of fire.

"Of course you didn't," Zimmerman continued, baiting the man. "That's just what I'll tell him. That you didn't say the message came from Holland. Or should I tell him that you said the message didn't come from Holland? Yeah, maybe that way is better. After all, we wouldn't want to confuse your boss, would we?"

"Look, you . . ." the gunman said, anger now replacing confusion. His eyes narrowed to slits, giving him the appearance of a pig with a potato for a nose. "I don't know what you're trying to pull, but—"

He never finished the sentence. As he drew closer and leaned over the table to face down the policeman, Zimmerman gave the underbraces of the table a violent kick, sending it heavily into the man's legs and pitching him forward. Before the hoodlum could regain his balance, Zimmerman was on his feet. With a deftness born of long experience and training, he snatched the gun with his left hand and brought his right fist down hard, like a sledge, on the base of the man's skull. As if in slow motion, the intruder slid backward off the table, dragged down by the weight of his own legs. A trail of blood smeared along the table, beginning at

143

the point where the blow had crushed his nose and ending at the table's edge.

Zimmerman watched his descent with interest before turning to his wife.

"Are you all right, Kath?"

Shivering uncontrollably, she nodded that she was.

As she came out of her shock, she looked at her husband in a new and different way. She had never before seen him perform as a policeman, and the violence with which he had reacted, followed by the false calm he now displayed, both intrigued and frightened her. The man on the floor groaned and tried to get to his knees. Zimmerman reached forward and placed a precise rabbit punch at the point where the gunman's neck met his left shoulder, sending him sprawling back into unconsciousness. Kathy winced as his face struck the floor.

The lieutenant strode to the telephone and lifted the receiver. His eyes never left the man on the floor. Dialing "four-one-one" with the hand that still held the gun, he waited patiently for the Information operator to answer.

"Information. May I help you?"

"Yes, operator. Give me the number of Thomas Holland, 2119 Hicks Street, Brooklyn."

There was a long pause before the operator spoke again.

"I'm sorry, sir, but that is an unlisted number."

Zimmerman grimaced with annoyance. "Operator, this is official police business. My name is Lieutenant Alfred Zimmerman, badge number 303097. You can verify my identity with Manhattan Homicide South, if you want."

The operator was not quite sure what to do. "My instructions are not to give out any unlisted numbers, sir," she finally said. "Would you like to speak to my supervisor?"

"Yes, if I must."

The phone clicked twice and burped once. Then another

144

voice came on the line.

"Yes, sir. May I help you? This is Miss Cully."

"This is Lieutenant Alfred Zimmerman, badge number 303097, NYPD. I'd like the number of Thomas Holland, 2119 Hicks Street, Brooklyn. The operator said it was unlisted."

"Lieutenant, I'm sure you can appreciate the position you're putting us in. Our customers pay us *not* to give out that information."

"This is urgent, miss. Police business."

"Very well, sir. What unit are you attached to?"

"Manhattan Homicide South."

"What is the name of your captain?"

"McIlhenny," Zimmerman answered, beginning to worry that Miss Cully might call the captain to verify his identity, and start a stream of questions about why he was investigating his brother's murder again. He was sure that Snyder had already reported his feelings to his commanding officer, either personally or through his own captain.

"One moment, please, sir." He heard paper rustling. "Very well, that would be captain Peter McIlhenny?" she asked.

"No, his first name is Michael," he answered.

"Right!" she announced. "Now let me get you that number. Thomas Holland on Hicks Street in Brooklyn, wasn't it?"

"That's right."

There was another short pause as she consulted the appropriate sheets.

"That number is 555, 3806, sir."

"KLondike 5, 3806," he repeated.

"Yes, sir."

He dialed that number as soon as he could get another dial tone.

"Holland residence," the butler intoned.

"Put Holland on," Zimmerman demanded. "This is Lieutenant Zimmerman."

"One moment, please, sir," the unflappable servant said automatically.

"Yes, Lieutenant," Holland said when he came on the line, "What can I do for you?" There was a note of annoyance in his voice, giving the impression that he felt having to talk to any civil servant under the rank of commissioner or judge was beneath him.

"I've got one of your boys here, Olanda. A pig-faced slob with a nose like a rummy. What do you want me to do with him?"

"I beg your pardon?"

"Wait a minute," Zimmerman said. He went to the prostrate intruder and, holding the gun carefully in his left hand, reached into his hip pocket with the other. He drew out the man's wallet and flipped through it quickly until he came to the driver's license, then returned to the phone.

"Henry Robinson, according to his driver's license." He riffled through the wallet again and stopped when he came to a stiff paper card that identified the man as an employee of Algonquin in the Security section.

"I also have this Algonquin Corporation I.D. card."

"Mr. Zimmerman," Holland said wearily. "If an Algonquin employee has gotten himself into some kind of trouble with the police, I suggest you talk to the personnel manager. Personally, I never heard of the man."

"Wrong. No personnel manager. You. He told me that you sent him here to try to scare me off."

There was an extended silence at the other end of the line.

"He told you that?"

"Not in so many words, but he's not overly bright, is he? I got him to admit it."

Holland sighed. "Well, Lieutenant, what do you want from me?" There was resignation in his voice.

"You've got it wrong, buddy. The question seems to be, What do you want from me?"

"I don't follow you," Holland replied.

"Look," Zimmerman said. "I'm not bothering you. You're bothering me. All I did was call on you once to ask some questions. You gave me the answers. Fine. Now that should have been the end of it. But instead, when I got in my car to drive back to my office, I found that your clown here had been playing games with my steering and brakes. Now if you had really wanted to kill me, you would have done it. You wouldn't have just tampered with my car enough to cause a bad accident.

"Then this crumb showed up here tonight, scared hell out of my wife, and started waving a gun around in front of my nose. Again, if you had wanted me dead, he just could have started shooting. So obviously you want something else. If you can tell me what it is, I might be able to oblige."

There was a short silence as Zimmerman caught his breath and Holland collected his thoughts.

"I see," Holland said. "Well, believe me, Lieutenant, there isn't anything I want from you. Nothing at all. And I can assure you that I knew nothing of these harassments. All I want is to be left alone—by the police, by you, by everybody. I'm just a simple businessman and I just want to be left alone to conduct my business."

"I hope that's all you want," Zimmerman said. "Because that much I'm willing to go along with. Believe me, I couldn't care less about what you choose to call your business. You succeeded in doing something tonight that very few other people have done—you got me really mad. When I'm on duty and I have to look at punks who think they're big men because they have guns, that's one thing. But

147

when somebody invades my home, that's something else entirely.

"Now I'll tell you what I'm going to do, Holland. I'm going to turn loose this thug you sent over. I'll keep the gun, of course. He might hurt himself with it. But I'm going to keep my eyes open. If I ever see him, or you, or any of your other hired hands anywhere near me or my family again, then I'm going to pull this crud in and start questioning him. I don't think I have to tell you how long he'll last under interrogation before he starts filling us in on everything he knows about your operation. It only took a couple of minutes for him to lead me to you tonight.

"And also—if, by any chance, Robinson should turn up dead in some alley, you'd better start worrying for real. Remember, I can supply a beautiful motive for you to want him dead. You'll feel heat that you never believed existed. Have I made myself clear?"

"Perfectly clear, Lieutenant," Holland answered. "Will there be anything else?" he asked with an air of false bravado.

"Now that you mention it, there will be something else. First your boys murdered my brother, now your Champlain Insurance Company won't pay on his life-insurance claim. They're giving my lawyer some song and dance about it being possible that my sister-in-law could have committed the murder, and they can withhold payment until she proves otherwise. We both know better, don't we? Believe me, I'll dig so deep into your organization that the termites will squirm if I have to in order to get that claim paid off. I don't think you want that."

"You have to understand," Holland argued, "that Algonquin is a very large company with many diverse parts. It's no exaggeration when I say that there are occasions when literally one hand doesn't know what the other hand is do-

148

ing. I can assure you that this is the first I've heard of any life-insurance claim."

"That's not my problem. Straighten it out!" Zimmerman commanded.

"I'll do what I can," Holland agreed.

Zimmerman hung up the phone with a feeling of accomplishment. His wife, having regained much of her composure, looked at him expectantly as she awaited his report.

Instead of describing the telephone conversation, however, he asked Kathy to get some facial tissue. She returned a moment later and handed him a wad. He slipped the revolver into his pocket and went to the kitchen sink, where he soaked the porous paper. Returning to his downed prey, Zimmerman slapped the soggy mass in his face. Spluttering and groaning, Robinson returned to consciousness.

"Hold this under your nose to stop the bleeding," Zimmerman advised as the man climbed to his feet. Robinson obeyed automatically. Taking him by the shoulder, the lieutenant led him to the door.

"I want you to understand something, Robinson," he said as the two men stood in the hallway. "I know who you are and I've got you whenever I want you." He handed back the wallet and with his other hand took the pistol from his pocket. "Anytime I want, I can slap a charge of 'assault with a deadly weapon' on you. And I've got your little Saturday night special here as evidence, as well as a witness. If I ever see your face again, that's exactly what I will do. You look as if you've been in trouble before, so it won't go easy. You'd probably draw the maximum sentence.

"So if you really want to do about ten years on the State, come back around someday. Otherwise, I never want to see you again. Do you get my message?"

Robinson nodded dumbly as he backed away in fear, anxious to get out of there as quickly as he could.

Without another word, Zimmerman turned and stepped back into his apartment, slamming the door behind him. He glanced at his wristwatch.

"Damn," he said as he resumed rubbing his wrist, "I've already missed the first inning of the ball game."

CHAPTER 25

"I CAN'T BELIEVE IT," the lawyer announced, shaking his head in bewilderment as he addressed Zimmerman and his sister-in-law. He had summoned them to his office to bring them up to date on some "startling new developments" in their insurance case.

"I've been in this business for a long time, but nothing like this has ever happened to me before. And with Champlain Insurance Company, yet."

Zimmerman merely smiled politely, but his brother's widow was confused.

"You seemed pleased, Mr. Finkle," she said, "and I supposed that means that something good has happened with our claim. But I'd really appreciate it if you'd tell us what it is."

"I'm sorry, Mrs. Zimmerman. I suppose I'm savoring an unexpected success at this point in the game. You'll have to forgive my little indulgence." His moustache twitched with happiness, and his eyes sparkled like those of a little boy who has just received a report card with all A's.

"I received a telephone call from Champlain Insurance Company today. Now, as I told your brother-in-law"—he gestured to the policeman—"and as I later explained to you when we finally met, I had anticipated that this would be a long-drawn-out business, with us eventually accepting a fairly high settlement. I never held out any hope of full payment, now did I?"

He went on without waiting for an answer.

"Well, I'm happy to say I was wrong. When they called me today, they played a tune I've never heard from them before. They started by asking me what we'd take to settle the claim. Now that, in itself, is unheard of with insurance companies—any insurance company, not just shyster outfits like Champlain. Usually, they make some ridiculously low offer, then wait for us to come up with a counterfigure. Then we go back and forth six or seven times until we reach a compromise acceptable to both parties. So you can imagine how surprised I was when they came right out and asked me for a figure. Well, this was enough to set me off, so I told them that it was a hundred thousand or we'd take them to court. I reasoned, as it turned out correctly, that something had them running scared, and I'd play it to the hilt. I don't, for the life of me, know what it is they're afraid of, though."

He looked from Barbara Zimmerman to the policeman for an explanation, but both returned his gaze without giving any hint of knowing what could have caused the turnabout.

"Whatever it was, though," Finkle continued, "it really had them on the ropes. The guy told me that he'd have to check with his boss—a standard line, by the way—and call me back. I figured another couple of weeks would go by and they'd come back with a partial offer. But no! Not twenty minutes went by before the guy was back on the phone.

"This time, he made the standard 'widow's mite' offer. He said they'd pay the full amount but it would be monthly installments of one hundred dollars until the hundred thousand was exhausted. He started giving me the old story about it being easier for a poor widow to manage her money when it came in that way, and all that stuff.

"Well, I let him know that we wouldn't consider it. Needless to say, he didn't like that one bit. Anyway, to make a long story short, he told me he'd have to check with his boss and call me back again.

"Exactly fourteen minutes later—I clocked it—they called back. This time it was another fellow who said he was the first man's boss. He tried me again on the widow's mite, just to make sure that his flunky hadn't gotten the deal garbled somehow. I told him that the other guy had made it perfectly clear, and that we were rejecting the offer and wanted the whole sum, one hundred thousand dollars in cash, or we'd take them to court.

"He hemmed and hawed for a minute, but when he realized that there was no way he was going to get me to budge, he backed down. He gave in. He said we'd have their check by the end of the week! Can you believe it?"

For the first time since her husband's death, Barbara Zimmerman was beaming. Expressions of gratitude welled forth from her throat like a cup running over.

Alfred Zimmerman, although pleased with this speedy action from the insurance company, was less than ebullient.

"Uh, Barney . . ." he began, "about your fee . . ."

"You might at least thank me first," the lawyer answered, his enthusiasm now tempered by a businesslike air. He regarded Zimmerman coolly. "Okay," he conceded. "You're right. I've already considered that aspect. As much as I'd like to think that the insurance company heard that I was on the case and my reputation frightened them into an early settlement, I'm not really that conceited. I don't know what made them do what they're doing, but I know it wasn't I. I'd feel like a crook myself if I held you up for my full fee. I didn't do that much work. So I'll settle for ten thousand. Okay?"

"That still seems high," Zimmerman answered. "After all, it's only been a few weeks since I first spoke to you about this case. A little research, a couple of meetings with us, and a few phone calls—that's really all you did, isn't it? And you yourself told us that you don't know why the insurance company came through so quickly. You admitted that it wasn't really through your actions."

The lawyer realized that the policeman had argued him into a corner.

"Did you ever consider becoming a trial lawyer, Lieutenant?" he asked rhetorically. He held up his hands in mock surrender.

"Okay, okay, you win. Five thousand."

"Two thousand," the policeman counterbid.

"Two thousand dollars?" Finkle seemed alarmed at the absurdity of the figure. "Why, I get more than that for handling . . ." He searched his mind for something ridiculously simple but was unable to came up with anything. He looked into Zimmerman's eyes to try to establish whether the policeman's offer could be raised. All he could perceive was unyielding determination.

"Oh, all right. Two thousand dollars. But I feel like I'm giving my services away. The workman is worthy of his hire, you know."

"Two thousand dollars is a lot of money," Zimmerman reminded him.

"Yes, I suppose it is in this case," Finkle allowed. The haggling over, he turned his attention back to Barbara.

"Now this is quite a bit of money you'll be getting. Ninety-eight thousand dollars net. I would strongly advise you to obtain the services of an investment counselor. Their standard fee, if you're interested,"—he shot a slightly dirty look at the policeman—"is one half of one percent, plus a percentage of the commissions on buying and selling investments."

"I don't know anybody like that," she said, looking a little worried. "Could you recommend . . ."

"As it happens, Mrs. Zimmerman, I perform those services myself for some of my clients. But I'm not trying to hustle you into anything. After all, we don't even have the insurance check yet. There's time to think about how you're going to invest it. I strongly advise you to get professional investment help, though, even if you choose to use somebody other than myself."

He got up and walked around his desk toward them. Zimmerman and Barbara rose and moved slowly toward the door.

"You'll have to excuse me now," the attorney added, "I have to be in court on another case shortly." He extended his hand, which they both shook. He smiled benevolently. "Believe me, Mrs. Zimmerman, I wish all my cases ended as well as this one has." Turning to face Zimmerman, he said, "I get this feeling that you know more about what happened here than you're letting on. Someday you'll have to tell me."

The policeman smiled like a little boy with a secret.

"Maybe someday," he conceded. "When we've both retired and we run into each other on the beach in Florida. In the meantime, it's better that you don't know."

The lawyer smiled and shrugged his shoulders as he ushered them through the door.

"I'll look forward to that, Lieutenant. I'll look forward to that."

CHAPTER 26

THE LIEUTENANT and Barbara squirmed into the taxicab they had hailed in front of the lawyer's office and endeavored to make themselves comfortable in the cramped back seat. Zimmerman thought back longingly to the old DeSoto cabs which, by comparison, were as large as living rooms.

"You really didn't have to come with me," Barbara said as the taxi pulled away from the curb and merged into traffic.

"I know I didn't *have* to," Al replied. "Perhaps I wanted to."

"It's far out of your way, though. All the way to Brooklyn and back."

"Don't worry about it."

They rode in silence until the cab turned onto the Manhattan Bridge. Then Al noticed that his sister-in-law was smiling wryly.

"What's the matter?" he asked.

"Nothing, Al. I was just thinking—look who's becoming a coupon clipper."

"Well, at least you're provided for. You won't have to worry about money anymore. You'll have a nice income coming in." The thought crossed his mind that perhaps Finkle had backed down as easily as he had on his fee because he was trading an immediate gain for a lifelong client. As Barbara's investment counselor, he would be good for

156

commissions and percentages for a long, long time.

She sighed sadly and grew serious. "You know, Al, it's really too bad Arnie couldn't have lived to see this."

"Lived to see you collect on his life insurance?" Zimmerman asked incredulously.

"No. Lived to see us get all this money. That was always his problem, you know. Lack of money. Oh, he made a living, I suppose. At least we never really had to go without any of the necessities. But that was never enough for him. He's the only person I ever knew whose one passion in life was to be rich. Not just comfortable, either. We could have been that many times—people offered him some pretty good jobs through the years, you know. But if he couldn't see how the job was going to lead to the presidency of the company, and quickly at that, he'd turn it down. He lived for the day when he'd be rolling in money. And he really believed that if he kept trying with his big deals and his racetrack friends, he'd make it.

"A hundred thousand dollars," she declared. "He'd have liked that."

She coughed to cover the fact that her voice was becoming choked.

"Well, at least he saw to it that you'll never have money problems again," Zimmerman offered weakly.

"Yes," she agreed. "That was his way, all right. I remember when he took that policy out—it was about two and a half years ago. When I finally got him to tell me what the monthly premiums were, I thought I'd die. We needed the money for clothes for the kids, for new furniture, for a million and one things more important to me, and he took out all that insurance. 'At least, when I die, you'll have money,' he said. That was the only time we ever discussed the insurance. That's why I was so shocked when the company only offered eleven thousand dollars at first. I knew that he had a hundred thousand. It was almost a point of pride with him. It's strange, but thinking back, I don't think he tossed and turned so much in his sleep after he took out that policy. It was as if a burden had been lifted from his mind. And believe me, he used to be the world's most restless sleeper. But then you probably knew that—you two used to share a room when you were kids, didn't you?"

"Yeah. He was always the active one," Zimmerman replied, yet he could not recall his brother having been a restless sleeper as a child.

"Speaking of Arnie and money," Barbara said, changing the subject somewhat, "I know he owed you quite a lot of money. He didn't tell me too much, but I sort of figured where the money was coming from when it miraculously appeared from time to time. Now that I've got it, I want to pay you back. Arnie would have wanted me to."

"Forget it," Zimmerman told her.

"No. It must be three or four thousand dollars. I can't have you out of that kind of money on our account. Particularly now that I have some money."

Her understatement of the amount surprised him. In truth, Arnold Zimmerman had borrowed closer to twenty thousand dollars from his brother through the years.

"You're going to need it for the kids," he said. "Besides, a hundred thousand dollars—actually, ninety-eight thousand —may sound like a lot, but you're going to need every cent of it. Remember, if you're lucky, you'll be getting an income of seven or eight thousand a year. That's enough to live on comfortably enough, but it certainly isn't any great riches. Besides, before you know it, the kids will be in college and you'll really need it."

"I insist, Al. Arnie would have wanted me to pay you back."

Zimmerman suppressed a sigh. This conversation was beginning to get the best of him. He had neatly compartmentalized his brother's death, and had tried not to think about Arnie as a person, but rather as a case to investigate. The discussion of his personality was beginning to strike too close to home.

"I said 'forget it,' and I meant 'forget it,'" he said brusquely. "I don't want to talk about it anymore."

"There, you see," she cried triumphantly. "You are annoyed about all the money that Arnie borrowed from you. I insist on paying you back. Now how much was it, exactly?"

"I don't know, Barbara. I didn't keep a set of books on my brother. And I don't want any of your money. As I said, you're going to need it yourself."

"Right is right, Al. And I'm not going to drop the subject until we come to some agreement that includes my paying you back."

"All right," he finally agreed. "I'll tell you what. After your kids have graduated from college, then you pay me back the money. When the kids are out on their own and you don't need the big income anymore."

She considered this for a moment.

"All right, Al," she said, her voice deeper. "If that's the way you want it. Now how much should I figure on?"

"Oh, three or four thousand. Like you said."

She was relieved at her elimination of another responsibility, and sat back in the cab seat. For the remainder of the drive to her door, she talked about nothing more serious than how cool the weather had become and what the chances were for a nice Indian summer that year.

His replies had been largely monosyllabic, as he was deep in thought.

CHAPTER 27

HE WAS STILL lost in his thoughts as he walked from his brother's house toward the subway station after dropping off his sister-in-law. As he stepped down off the curb and crossed the street, before rounding the corner which would lead him directly to the train, a plan of action was beginning to form in his mind. He did not come out of his pensive daze until he found himself in front of the change booth on the street level of the station.

"I don't want to take the subway," he announced to the surprised woman in the booth.

"So don't!" she called after him as he turned and went back out to the street. "So who's making you?"

Back on the street, he walked directly to a waiting taxi and piled into its rear seat.

"Do you know where the police headquarters is on Wilson Avenue?" he asked the driver.

"Do I know where the police headquarters is on Wilson Avenue?" the driver repeated, glancing at his fare in the mirror. "I'm a cab driver, ain't I?" He pulled out from his position in the shade of the overhead train platform and cut quickly into traffic. "I get tickets, don't I? I got to pay the tickets, don't I? Or else I lose my hack license. Do I know where it is!"

Turning left at Ocean Avenue and slipping smoothly into the flowing stream of cars traveling the artery, the driver again looked at Zimmerman by means of the rear-view mirror. Seeing that the passenger was preoccupied, he asked, "You got a ticket? Is that why you want to go to the police station?"

"Huh?" Zimmerman asked, not having paid attention to the chauffeur.

"What a racket those cops got," the driver continued. "Look at all the dough they collect just on traffic tickets. I mean, they get fifteen bucks just on a parking violation. And now it's going up to twenty-five. Jesus, twenty-five bucks for a parking ticket.

"I got one myself about two weeks ago. What a lot of crap, too. I stopped in front of Wolf's—the cafeteria over on Newkirk—to get myself some lunch. I'll tell you, I start work at five thirty in the morning and I work until six o'clock at night. Six days a week. So by about eleven thirty in the morning, I'm pretty hungry, see. Well, I went into Wolf's—they got good pastrami there, by the way, real good—to get myself a cup of coffee and a sandwich. Tongue on rye with Russian dressing. My stomach was a little upset the night before—this damn traffic will give you an ulcer, I swear—so I had the tongue instead of the pastrami. They got good tongue, too, if you want something a little milder than the pastrami, if you know what I mean."

He swung his cab hard to the right to get onto Flatbush Avenue, where the two streets merged at the edge of Prospect Park. In so doing, he came within three inches of side-swiping a delivery truck whose driver didn't seem quite sure whether or not to turn. Zimmerman gripped the armrest tightly to keep from losing his balance as the cab swerved and swayed.

"Idiot!" the driver cursed. "The way some people drive. They don't know where the hell they're going, but they expect the whole world to get out of their way.

"Like I was saying," he continued when he had the car back under control, "I stopped in for a sandwich. I mean a man's entitled to eat, ain't he? I couldn't have been in there more than ten minutes. I hadn't even finished half my sandwich. And I saw this damn cop out on the sidewalk looking my cab over. I could see him through the window. I always take a seat where I can keep my eye on the cab. The way this city's going, you can't take your eyes off anything or somebody'll steal it or slash your tires or something. So I saw this cop looking at my cab. I didn't even finish my sandwich. I put it down and ran out of there—I tossed a couple of bucks to the cashier on the way out—I didn't even get a check for the food. But by the time I got there, he was already writing. Or at least he had his pad out and he was just going to start writing the ticket.

" 'What's the matter, officer?' " I asked him.

" 'You're parked illegally,' " he said.

"So I told him that I had just gone inside for a quick sandwich, and I asked him if he'd like to join me. I'd pay. 'No thank you,' he said, 'I just ate.' So by this time, I knew what he wanted. I took out my wallet and took out a five and just sort of stood there looking at it. 'Well, then,' I said, 'maybe you'll let me pay for your dinner?'

"Jesus, you'd think I insulted him or something. 'Put your money away, cabby,' he told me, 'before I have to charge you with attempted bribery!" Attempted bribery! Me! And he wrote me the ticket.

"Son of a bitch! You know what he wanted, don't you? He wanted more money. Five bucks wasn't good enough for him!"

The driver had become quite excited in the telling of his story, and Zimmerman was relieved when they turned a corner and he saw the police station looming ahead, the largest building on the block.

"So what did the sons of bitches ticket you for?" the driver asked as he slowed his vehicle in approaching the station.

"I don't have any ticket to pay," Zimmerman told him.

"No? Then why are you going here?" the driver asked, his curosity piqued.

"I'm a cop," the lieutenant answered with a smile as he handed the driver the exact fare, with no tip. He enjoyed the shocked expression on the driver's face and was still laughing when he entered the main hall and waved greetings to the desk sergeant. His smile didn't fade until he entered the offices of the Homicide squad.

CHAPTER 28

LIEUTENANT DAVID SNYDER regarded his Manhattan South counterpart with surprise when he entered the room. After their last encounter in Zimmerman's office, he had not expected to see him again until some future training class or Chief of Detectives meeting.

"Well, well, well," Snyder mocked, "Look who's here. The master detective himself. Who are you today, Philo Vance or Clark Kent? You're certainly not the Thin Man." He pointed to Zimmerman's ample waistline.

"What can I do for you today?" he asked, more serious but with a definite cutting edge on his voice.

"Okay, Duke," Zimmerman said humbly. "I had that coming. I've been stepping on your toes pretty regularly lately, and I figure I owe you an apology. So I apologize."

Zimmerman's new attitude caught Snyder off guard. He stared at his colleague for a moment and then, in a gentler voice, said, "Sit down, Al. You want some coffee?"

Zimmerman seated himself, but he waved off the coffee. The two men sat looking at each other for a moment. Finally, Snyder said, "Okay. Your apology is accepted. Believe me, it wasn't my intention to be so rough on you, either. I can appreciate what you've been going through, what with your brother being murdered. But you have to appreciate that that fact, as regrettable as it is, doesn't give you or any of us the right to throw away the book and act like television private eyes. We've got boundary lines, and

164

they make sense. A man can't work on a case involving a member of his own family, and maybe now you'll agree that that makes sense, too. You seem a lot more reasonable today." He smiled.

Zimmerman returned the smile, but he offered no statement to support Snyder's efforts to say that he had been right all along.

Again, the two policemen found themselves staring at each other. Snyder's gaze broke first.

"Al, I get a very uncomfortable feeling that you didn't come here just to apologize. Maybe I'm too suspicious, but I think you want something else from me. Why don't you tell me what it is and get it over with?"

Zimmerman looked embarrassed. "You're right, Duke. I do want something." He saw Synder's face darken with apprehension. "I'd like to take one last look at my brother's file—please."

Snyder drew in his breath and was about to loose another tantrum, but Zimmerman cut him off before he could speak. "Duke! Please. Before you start yelling again, hear me out. This is the end of it. The end. I'm not snooping around in your territory anymore. I simply have to check out some facts before I can really lay my mind to rest about my brother's murder. Please, Duke. I'm not trying to find the killer. This is for me. A personal favor from you to me. Please let me see the file."

The policeman behind the desk raised his arms to the sky and pronounced: "Why me, Lord? Why me?" He rose to his feet and stared at Zimmerman briefly, then turned and strode to his filing cabinet. Without a word, he slid the metal drawer open and searched with his fingers until he found what he was looking for. He pulled the file out of its slot and slammed the drawer shut. Slapping the file down on the desk in front of Zimmerman, he walked to the door.

"Let me know when you're finished and I can get some

work done around here," he said as he left his office and closed the door, leaving Zimmerman alone to study the file.

Less than thirty minutes passed before Zimmerman opened the door and asked Lieutenant Snyder to return. He handed his host the file and he entered the office.

"Well," Zimmerman said with an air of finality, "that's it. I'm off your back. Thanks for the use of the office."

"Did you find what you were looking for?" Snyder asked curious.

"Yep," Zimmerman replied smugly. "Everything checks out."

"Aren't you going to let me in on it? You didn't seem too sure that DiBennidetto was your man the last time I saw you. Now you look like the cat that swallowed the canary."

"Duke, I'll tell you what I've found under one condition —you keep the case closed, with DiBenidetto listed as the probable killer."

"What do you mean 'probable'? Holland told you he was. What more do you need?"

"First give me your word. It can't make any difference now, except on a strictly personal level. What I mean to say is that the case is already marked 'closed,' and to reopen it could only cause unnecessary pain to my brother's family."

"All right, Al. If, after you've told me what you think you've found, I agree that there is no good to be served by reopening the case, I'll let things stand as they are. Fair enough?"

"Fair enough," Zimmerman agreed.

"Then what have you got that convinces you that DiBennidetto didn't murder Arnold Zimmerman?"

Zimmerman took a deep breath before he began.

"Well, we can start with the fact that my brother wasn't murdered!"

"Not murdered?" Snyder challenged. "Half his head was

blown off, for God's sake. How can you say he wasn't murdered? First you drive us crazy investigating this case yourself and blowing our investigation of a top Mafia leader. And now you say he wasn't murdered after all?"

Zimmerman held up his hand as a stop signal. "Duke, maybe you'd better let me tell this my way. We're not going to get anywhere if you interrupt me every time I say anything."

"Well, you're not going to convince me that a man was shot in the back of the head at close range by accident," Snyder said, "but go on and try. I've got the time if you do." His look dared Zimmerman to sell him on a new approach to the problem.

Zimmerman's mouth turned up at the corners in a patient smile. "Hear me out, Duke. Hear me out."

Snyder nodded affirmatively.

"I'll explain this to you piece by piece and you can see if what I tell you doesn't answer all the open questions in the file. That's why I had to go through it again, you see.

"First, let's take some facts. My brother's body was found on his front stoop. He had been shot in the back of the head—actually, at the point where the base of the skull joins the neck. The coroner said death was instantaneous, right?"

"Yeah."

"Okay. Now one of the things the coroner couldn't explain was the angle of the bullet. We never did come up with an explanation for that. The bullet traveled in a downward path, which meant that, considering the elevation of the steps, the killer would have had to be a giant. DiBennidetto was five foot ten. He hardly qualified, right?"

Synder, obviously intrigued, sat forward in his chair. "Go on," he said.

"Set that piece of information aside for a moment, and let's go on to something else. The coroner also told us that my brother's right wrist had been sprained very shortly before his death. Do you remember that?"

"Yes," Snyder said. "As I recall, he said it looked as if his arm had been twisted behind him. We assumed that the killer held him in a hammerlock and probably shot him while he was still holding on to his arm. The powder burns, if you recall, indicated that he was shot at extremely close range."

"Yes," Zimmerman agreed. "The close range was borne out by the traces of blood on the murder weapon as well. And the fact that the sprain wasn't very severe could be explained by twisting as you described. But let's file that information, too, until I've listed all the pieces of this puzzle. Then you'll see how they all fit together."

"All right," Snyder said impatiently. "But let's get on with it."

"Next, let's talk about the motive for murder. My brother owed some money to the mob—or at least to its loan sharks. He was overdrawn at his bank when he died, so we can assume that he couldn't pay them off. The amount he owed them was something in the neighborhood of two thousand dollars.

"Your assumption was that the killing was so typical of a Syndicate-type assassination that it was one. Also, the fact that he was in arrears to the Organization in paying off his debts gave the motive. They killed him as a warning to other deadbeats. We've both seen them do things like that before, and we both assumed that they had done it again. But we were wrong."

"Holland told you as much," Snyder protested. "He admitted that one of their boys, that DiBennidetto person, had killed your brother for exactly those reasons. You told me so! Weren't you telling me the truth about what Holland told you?"

"Of course I was, Duke. That's what he told me. But what I'm saying now is that Holland was wrong. He made the same assumptions we did—that, because the assassination was fairly typical of the organization's modus operandi, it was one of its members who had done it.

"But, and this is a very important point, he also told me that DiBennidetto denied it to the end. That was why they killed him—for lying to them. They were so convinced that he had killed my brother—he had, in fact, been assigned to lean on him a little—that they assumed he had simply gone too far in his zeal to collect. Add to this that they believed he and some of his cronies from other branches of the Organization were thinking about going into business for themselves, and it starts to have a logical pattern. I can understand it fooling them. Let me put it this way: they knew he had been seeing some people he shouldn't have been seeing. Then he told what to them was an obvious lie. Adding one and one, they decided that they couldn't trust him anymore, so they got rid of him.

"He was in a bad position, though, DiBennidetto was. He was an innocent man forced to prove his innocence. The Mafia doesn't exactly believe that a man is innocent until proved guilty, you know. So his dilemma was, should he lie to them and admit doing something he hadn't done, or should he tell the truth and take his chances that they'd believe him? His training in the Organization had taught him that to lie to his bosses was unthinkable, a cardinal sin. So he told them the truth, that he hadn't killed my brother. The only problem was that they didn't believe him. You know the result."

"I hear what you're saying, Al," Snyder said. "But you still haven't answered some pretty important questions. If DiBennidetto didn't kill your brother, who did? Or do you still insist that it was some kind of freak accident?"

"I never said it was an accident," Zimmerman said. "You jumped to that conclusion when I told you that it wasn't murder."

169

"Well, if it wasn't murder, and it wasn't an accident, what the hell is left?" Snyder demanded.

Zimmerman looked at him calmly, like a teacher about to reveal a great truth. "Suicide," he said.

Snyder thought about this for a moment. The unconsidered possibility had stopped him in his tracks, forcing him to recoup his thoughts. Finally, after mulling this new alternative over in his mind until it sank in, he rejected it.

"I can't buy it, Al. What you're trying to tell me is that a man shot himself through the back of the head on his own doorstep, didn't leave a note, never hinted his intention to anybody, just because he owed some loan shark a couple of thousand bucks. No. No. It's too weak. I can't buy it."

"Okay," Zimmerman offered, "Then I'll prove it to you, step by step. Believe me, it's the only explanation where everything falls into place.

"What kind of gun do you use?" Zimmerman began by asking.

"A thirty-eight police special," Snyder answered, puzzled by the question. "Why?"

"How long is the barrel?"

"Four inches, but I don't know what you're getting at."

"Unload your gun and give it to me," Zimmerman said.

Shaking his head to indicate his confusion, Snyder did as he had been told, carefully removing the six brass-cased bullets from his weapon and handing the empty gun to his colleague across the desk.

Zimmerman flipped open the cylinder and inspected the sidearm to make sure it was empty. He clicked the cylinder shut once he was satisfied.

"Watch this," he told Snyder. "The four-inch barrel on your gun makes it roughly the same size as a Luger." Placing his right hand, which held the gun, over his head, he carefully brought the weapon down behind his head so that, with his elbow pointing straight up in the air, the muzzle of the gun touched the base of his skull.

"Come around behind me and look at the angle of the barrel in relation to my head and neck."

Lieutenant Snyder got up and moved behind Zimmerman. "It points slightly downward," he observed.

"About the same angle as the shot that killed my brother?" Zimmerman asked.

"I guess so."

"Good. Now look at the position of my right hand and wrist."

"It's weird," Snyder said, "all twisted around."

"Right. Now when was the last time you were on the firing range?"

"Why are you asking that now? About a month ago," Snyder revealed.

"How did your hand feel afterward?"

"Oh, I see what you're getting at. Yes, you're right. It was a little sore. The kick of the gun." Snyder was beginning to pick up the trend of Zimmerman's thinking.

"That's right. And if you or I, who are used to firing pistols from a proper position, come away with a sore wrist, how do you think the recoil would affect someone who was in the first place not used to it and who, secondly, was holding the gun in a twisted position like this?"

"Okay. You've made your point," Snyder conceded. "If the gun had been held that way, it could account for both the unusual angle of the bullet's path and for a slightly sprained wrist."

Zimmerman handed the pistol back to its owner.

"The suicide theory is the only one that I've thought about that accounts for all the little details. For example, the gun was found in the bushes a few feet away from the body. It could have fallen there after being fired. But what kind of professional killer would dispose of the murder weapon so near the scene of the crime? Even though it was an unregistered firearm, and of a type that would have been very difficult to trace ownership of, a professional would have hidden it somewhere or dumped it in the river or down a sewer. Also, there were smudges of prints on the gun's clip—no good clear fingerprints—just smudges. Again, if it had been a professional killer, he would certainly have wiped the prints—even the smudges—off the clip as well as the gun itself before disposing of the gun."

"That's pretty farfetched, Al," Snyder said. "What you're telling me is that your brother knew enough to wipe the gun clean before he picked it up, and then shot himself without getting any prints on it. How could he possibly have done that?"

Zimmerman thought for a moment, then said soberly; "The handkerchief. You told me that you found a handkerchief in the bushes, too. He used it to hold the gun while he shot himself. You said that the handkerchief turned out to be his. He wiped the gun clean before using it, but not being a professional gunman, he didn't think to clean the clip after he loaded the gun in the first place."

"I see," Snyder said, "but let me ask you this. Assuming everything you said is true and describes what really happened, why did he shoot himself in the back of the head? When people blow their brains out, they usually point the gun at their temple or forehead, or else put the gun barrel in their mouths and pull the trigger. Was he trying to make it look like murder? And if he was, why?"

That's probably part of it," Zimmerman acknowledged. "He probably did want it to look as if he had been murdered. Or at least, he was definitely trying to disguise the fact that he was committing suicide. I can't really tell you for sure why, but I can make a couple of good guesses. First, he was probably thinking about his life insurance, and he probably didn't know whether they'd pay off on a suicide. Second, he might have had some regrets about what he was doing—at least in terms of his family. He probably didn't want his kids to have to live with the stigma of a father who had killed himself, and he didn't want his wife to go through the guilt feelings of possibly having driven her husband to such a thing. I can't say that's what he was thinking. We'll never know, I suppose. But that kind of reasoning would have been in keeping with his character, at least as I knew him. It would also explain why he didn't leave a suicide note.

"That covers why he tried to make it look like murder. But there's another aspect that backs this up. I couldn't expect you to know this, but my brother was once a medical student. The place where he shot himself was the one part of the body where a bullet would bring death almost instantaneously. People shot in the temple or forehead can live for hours, sometimes longer. Once in a while they even recover.

"At the point where the neck joins the base of the skull, on the other hand, death is immediate. The coroner confirmed that when I spoke to him a few weeks ago. He said my brother never felt a thing. As a former medical student, my brother would have known that."

"Okay, Al," Snyder conceded. "You've told me how it could have happened. But you still haven't told me why. You're right—maybe we jumped to a conclusion when we assumed from the start that your brother had been murdered. But even *you* didn't suspect that he might have committed suicide then. What changed your mind?"

"Actually, it isn't so much that I changed my mind: I'm just looking at the facts in a different way. When you come right down to it, the reasons for his suicide are identical to the reasons we had used for his murder. He owed money to the racketeers, there was no way he could pay them back, and he knew they were going to collect in one way or another.

"To go off on a tangent, maybe you really had to know my brother to understand that this was exactly the type of thing he would do. I admit I have you at an advantage, there. He *was* my brother.

"As far back as I can remember, he's been a born loser. Oh, you'd never know it to look at him or listen to him, but he was just one of those people for whom everything he touched turned sour. He always had an angle he was playing that was going to make him a millionaire, but the angle never worked, and he usually ended up worse off than he was when he started. If he had just concentrated on doing what he had to do without looking for ways to exploit a given situation, he probably would have done pretty well for himself. But that just wasn't his way. He never took a straight path to get from point A to point B. He had one of the world's truly devious minds.

"Let me tell you a little story about my brother when we were kids. It'll show you what I mean." Zimmerman grinned somewhat wistfully as he remembered his childhood.

"Like all kids, he occasionally did a bit of shoplifting—usually candy bars or something like that. Okay, most kids do it. You did didn't you? I know I snatched more than one Hershey bar when I was a kid."

Snyder admitted with some embarrassment that he had done the same.

"Guilty as charged, your Honor," he said with a little smile.

"Well, here's the difference. My brother had a system. He was about nine years old at the time. We had a cousin Harry who was, oh, maybe three or four, who also lived in the neighborhood. Arnie used to ignore him most of the time, but at one point, they were always together. I got curious about this—I was the older brother, remember—and I followed them once.

"They went into the neighborhood candy store together.

174

Arnie made a big show over selecting a comic book, keeping the proprietor busy, while the little kid filled his pockets with candy. He was wearing one of Arnie's old coats and it fit him like a tent, but in our neighborhood, everybody wore hand-me-downs, so there wasn't anything unusual about that. Harry must have stolen twenty candy bars without showing a bulge in his pockets.

"They were too greedy, though, and the candy-store owner saw the little guy pocketing a Baby Ruth. He started yelling at him and calling him a thief.

"Here's where Arnie's instincts really came into play. Before our cousin could be made to empty his pockets and return the candy, Arnie ran over to him and slapped him half across the store. Then Arnie started hitting him and yelling at him that he was going to tell his mother and she was going to beat the hell out of him. Arnie reached into one of the kid's pockets and took out two or three candy bars, which he made a big production of putting back. Then he led Harry out by his ear.

"Well, to make a long story short, as soon as they got around the corner, the two of them broke up laughing. Arnie had made him give back a couple of candy bars, but he must have had two pounds of candy in his other pockets. The candy-store owner never told either of their parents, because he assumed that Arnie would take care of that. Besides, he saw Harry getting smacked right in his store. He never dreamed that Arnie had set the whole thing up."

Zimmerman paused as he grew more solemn.

"That may have been the last scheme that my brother dreamed up that really worked. When we were kids, he was an incurable optimist. Even later, as an adult, he sincerely believed that one of his plans was going to break right and he'd be on easy street.

"But maybe, by the time he reached his midforties, he finally realized that it simply wasn't going to happen. And he couldn't adjust to that. He couldn't admit that all these years he had been wrong and the hard-working wage slaves were right. He had spent the greater part of his life trying to prove the opposite.

"So he killed himself. Typically, it was well planned, though. He didn't want it to look like suicide, and he didn't tell anybody he was considering it. In the first place, he thought it might foul up his insurance, and secondly, it just wouldn't have been his way. If you had known him as I did, you'd see that I'm right."

Having finished his story, Zimmerman looked at Snyder, wondering whether the other lieutenant was accepting it.

Snyder was contemplating his hands, which he had folded in front of him on his desk. There was a period of silence before he spoke.

"Al," he began hesitantly. "I can see why you say that it would only hurt your brother's family, and not really do anybody any good to let this get out. But I don't think I can go along with keeping it quiet."

"Why not?"

"The insurance, Al. You said so yourself. He made it look like murder instead of suicide so that his wife could collect on the insurance. It would be dishonest to allow her to keep the money under those circumstances. We'd be accessories to defrauding his insurance company."

"No, we wouldn't." Zimmerman countered. "They'd have to pay anyway."

"On a suicide?"

"Sure. The only stipulation in most life insurance policies regarding suicide is that there is a two-year time limit from the time you take the policy out. Obviously, you can't take out a policy on Monday and kill yourself on Tuesday and expect them to pay. But it's equally obvious that it wouldn't be fair not to pay on a policy that someone has had for a long time, just because he committed suicide. Maybe in the interim he became deranged, or incurably ill and decided to end it as painlessly as possible. I won't say I approve of suicide, Duke, but there are times when it isn't as irrational as it might appear. No, the insurance companies won't hold up payment on cases like those.

"The way they protect themselves is with this two-year clause. If you commit suicide within the first two years of the policy, they won't pay. If it's longer than two years, though, they have to pay. And my brother's policy was in effect for almost three years—well, two and a half years, anyway—before he took his life."

"Two years?" Snyder asked. "I never heard of that."

"It's a standard clause in most life-insurance forms," Zimmerman said. "But just to make sure, I checked my brother's policy. It's there, all right."

"Hmmph," Snyder said thoughtfully. "Then I guess there really isn't any reason to set the record straight, just for the sake of setting it straight. I mean, after all, the case was considered closed before you walked in here today. I can't see any reason to reopen it and then reclose it, can you?"

Zimmerman smiled.

"After all," Snyder continued, talking himself into the decision, "you really haven't told me anything I can prove, have you? You came in with a theory, that's all. If it happens to make sense, all that proves is that you're a good cop. Still, you can't prove it with hard evidence, can you?"

"No, Duke, I can't," Zimmerman replied gratefully. "Now, if you'll pardon me, I think I've done enough of Brooklyn South's work for one year, and I've got plenty of my own to tackle."

Snyder smiled warmly. "Al, sorry about the heat I put on you. . . ."

Zimmerman raised his hand, signaling Snyder that no apologies were necessary. "Hey, buddy, if more apologies are called for, they should come from me for stepping out of my own territory."

The two men looked at each other self-consciously as Zimmerman extended his hand. Snyder hesitated, then reached out and shook it firmly.

Zimmerman was whistling as he bounced down the stairs on the balls of his feet and walked back out to the street. His smile didn't fade until he was halfway back to his own office.

CHAPTER 29

"WHAT'S EVERYBODY LOOKING AT?" Zimmerman asked as he strode through the anteroom to his office and was conscious of heads turning in his direction.

"You, Al," Sergeant Donofrio answered. "From the look on your face, you're back among the living."

Zimmerman looked at him quizzically.

"Sorry, Al," Donofrio corrected himself, embarassed. "That was a rotten choice of words."

"But accurate," Zimmerman stated flatly. "I have rejoined the living. For the first time since my brother's death, I really feel like my old self again. It's as if a weight had been lifted from my chest. Believe it or not, I feel great."

"What happened?" Donofrio asked, surprised at the ebullience of his lieutenant.

"Oh, nothing specific. It's just that the insurance company finally agreed to pay, and Snyder closed the case on my brother. I'll tell you, it's a big relief to know that I won't have to support my brother's family. A big relief. I really don't know where I would have gotten the money."

"Are you satisfied with Snyder's solution to your brother's case now?" Donofrio asked. "You didn't seem to think it held much water the last time we talked about it."

Zimmerman looked at his friend coolly, trying to decide whether to divulge his discovery and tell him that he had sold that story to the lieutenant in Brooklyn. He made up

179

his mind not to. The fewer people who knew the truth, the less the chance there was that the story might get back to his sister-in-law.

"Snyder's solution?" he asked rhetorically. "Snyder's solution was my solution. I told him what happened, didn't I? I got to thinking about it and I decided that inasmuch as I had solved the case for him, why shouldn't I accept my own findings? That makes sense, doesn't it?"

"Sure, Al," Donofrio said defensively. "You don't have to convince me, you know."

"Right," Zimmerman agreed, placing his hand on his friend's shoulder. "Look, I want to see the captain. Do you know if he's in his office?"

"If you turn around real slowly, you can rub noses with him." Donofrio grinned. While they had been talking, Captain McIlhenny had come out of his office and walked up behind them.

"Mac!" the lieutenant declared, punching his superior playfully in the shoulder. "Just the man I wanted to see. Got a minute?"

"Come on in, Al," McIlhenny invited, somewhat surprised at Zimmerman's exuberance. "You look like a kid who's found himself locked up in an ice-cream factory for the weekend."

Zimmerman slapped him on the back. "Well, I feel a lot better than that, Mac."

The two men entered the captain's office. "As it happens, I wanted to see you, too, Al," McIlhenny said, closing the door behind them.

"Oh?" Zimmerman asked, an air of apprehension cutting into his good spirits.

"Yeah. I just got a call from Snyder over in Brooklyn. Oh, maybe fifteen minutes ago. I don't know what's going on between you two guys, but it was certainly a change not to have him complaining."

Zimmerman's apprehension melted, leaving him smiling again.

"I really don't get it," McIlhenny continued. "All he said was that maybe he had been too harsh on you before when he was bitching about your not knowing the boundaries. He said that maybe if he had listened to you more in the first place, a lot of work could have been avoided."

McIlhenny stared at Zimmerman incredulously. "Would you mind telling me what the hell is happening now? All of a sudden, you two guys are bosom buddies, while yesterday you were at each other's throats. Did you see Snyder this morning, Al?"

"Yes I did, sir," Zimmerman replied slowly. Seeing that an explanation was expected by the captain, he continued; "I'll tell you the truth; I went to his office and apologized for having gotten in his way. I was in Brooklyn anyway, because I had to take my sister-in-law home. And I figured that I had been getting in Duke's hair quite a lot lately. I mean, I wouldn't have liked it very much if somebody started undercutting me in one of my investigations. At any rate, I recognized the fact that I had been way out of line with him and I apologized. He accepted my apology, and that's all there is to it."

"That's all you did—apologize?" McIlhenny asked suspiciously.

"That's all, sir," Zimmerman confirmed.

The captain stared at his lieutenant to see if any further information was forthcoming. Seeing that Zimmerman had said all he was going to say, McIlhenny decided to drop the subject.

"Well, Al. That must have been some apology! The way Snyder was going on, I wouldn't have been surprised if he suggested that I give you a medal. But be that as it may, I'm glad to see you feeling better. I don't mind telling you that you had me worried for a while. Good lieutenants are hard

181

to find. I wasn't looking forward to losing you."

Zimmerman was honestly embarrassed. "If you'll excuse me, sir," he began as he went toward the door.

"Sure, I know you've got a lot of catching up to do, Al. All I can really say is that it's good to have you back."

"Sir?"

"Oh, uh, yeah . . ." McIlhenny hesitated. "Uh, when you get your next pay check, don't worry about the sick-pay entry on the stub. I've been carrying you as being out on sick leave for almost two weeks now."

Zimmerman looked at the captain as the message sank in. He had been protected from an almost certain suspension by his captain's actions.

"Thank you, sir," he managed to mumble as his hand reached for the doorknob.

"Well," the captain elaborated, "if you want to take a busman's holiday and play detective while you're officially out sick, I don't see how I can be expected to know anything about it. Sick time is your own time. It's in the union contract. I'm your boss, and as far as I'm concerned, you were sick. If you chose to get out of your sickbed to do other things, that's your business."

"Thank you, Mac," Zimmerman repeated.

He did not see the captain break into a grin as he turned and left the office.

Standing in the anteroom once more, he paused to regain his composure. Sweeping his eyes across the room, he observed Detectives D'Angelo and Rumson elbow-resting on the water cooler, deep in some kind of chatter that was evoking laughter from them.

"Don't you guys have any work to do?" Zimmerman boomed. "Christ! If I'm not looking over your shoulders every minute, the whole place falls apart!"

The two detectives were shocked at first, but as their lieutenant disappeared into his office, they smiled at each other, signifying that it looked as if things were, indeed, back to normal.

"Donofrio!" Zimmerman called from the confines of his cubicle. "Where the hell is the Dunway file?"